THE SEA CRYSTAL
and Other Weird Tales

Praise for Susan Berliner's novels:

Corsonia

"I enjoyed very much how the main characters were portrayed as strong women with character and intent, not ditzy females clamoring about boys and makeup...The strength of the book is the tenacity and nerve of the lead characters. They are good role models, as girls who have the courage and desire to help those less fortunate." — Michael Nail, *Gimmethatbook*

"Well written and well paced." — *Julie's Book Review*

"Susan Berliner does it again! Rich imagination. Vivid imagery. Superb characterizations. Snappy dialogue, capturing very believable conversations between two teenage girls/best friends. So many twists and turns, it kept me wanting to read more, and I resented having to put it down for silly things like making dinner and bathing!" — Linda Commodore

"I finished reading *Corsonia* last night. I won't say it gave me nightmares, but my dreams were a bit more disturbing than usual! It was a great read, and gives the reader pause and makes you start thinking...could this actually happen? Not sure I ever want to find out!" — Judy Barnes

"Thoroughly enjoyable vacation read! The author has an innovative way of weaving factual incidents or occurrences into fast paced fiction." — Arlene Bender

The Disappearance

"*The Disappearance* is a terrific read...gratifying and suspenseful...for both young adults as well as adults. I highly recommend *The Disappearance*. Its message is thought-provoking and one young adults must keep in mind as they mature into adulthood." — *Night Owl Reviews (Top Pick)*

"I enjoy reading books with time travel - and this book took you back and forth constantly! It was done in such a way that had me almost believing it was really possible." — Michele Bodenheimer, *Miki's Hope*

"There are many modes of time travel, but this one takes the cake - so different from others I've read! Whatta way to travel - makes me slightly dizzy. This group of characters working together to bring down one culprit is so different, so eclectic; it's a wonder they ever met each other! But that's what makes it work! I love 'The Sting' all over again." — Lila L. Pinord

"I just loved this book! This is one of those books that will call you to pick it back up if you have the self-control to set it down for a moment. I was pulled in throughout the entire story because I could not wait to see what would happen next." — Dawn Fitzpatrick

Peachwood Lake

"It is a marvelous coming of age horror story."
— Night Owl Reviews (Top Pick)

"*Peachwood Lake* is another winner for new author Susan Berliner...Where else are you going to find a fish horror story that brings a young girl's life into focus?...I have no trouble recommending this book for the pre-teen/YA horror lover. Five out of five fairy kisses for this reader."
— Dottie Taylor, *Tink's Place*

"Great read. Fun and suspenseful. Best fish story since *Jaws*!"
— Peggy Derevlany

"This author creates characters with many layers and creatures that are so different from the average thriller type read that I can't wait to see what she comes up with next!" — Paula Davis

"I absolutely LOVED it! I can see this being a movie, a very awesome movie!" — Heather Marts

Dust

"Susan Berliner gives us an amazing mysterious supernatural story in *Dust*. It intrigues and holds the readers' attention, while pulling them in and not letting them put it down." *— Night Owl Reviews (Top Pick)*

"*Dust* picks you up and takes you on a whirlwind ride, pun intended, and doesn't let you go until the final climax...It's a great piece of escapist fiction and a book to easily get lost in." — Patricia Lane

"Susan Berliner's first novel is filled with drama, laughter, and engaging characters...As a high school English teacher, I plan to use this captivating novel with my students this year. I give *DUST* an A+!"
— Brittany Mott

"I was able to read this book in its entirety within just a few hours, which added to its cinematic qualities; it was like watching a movie in the afternoon...The language in the book is relatively simple and casual, easy to read, and doesn't contain much in the way of profanity, so it can be enjoyed by a wide age-group spectrum." — Andy S. Adams

THE SEA CRYSTAL
and Other Weird Tales

by Susan Berliner

Published by SRB Books

ISBN: 978-0-9839401-5-9

Cover design by Book Graphics
Book layout by Dianne Paulet
Author's photo by Rachel Leib Photography

Published April, 2016

Printed in the United States of America

Dedicated to storytellers and story writers everywhere—
especially young creative writers
who are no longer encouraged to use
their imaginations in school.
Keep on writing!

Thanks to all the friends, family, and readers
who continue to support my creative writing efforts
and special thanks to my husband, Larry,
who is always there for me.

"Short stories are tiny windows
into other worlds
and other minds
and other dreams.
They are journeys you can make
to the far side of the universe
and still be back in time for dinner."
– Neil Gaiman

INTRODUCTION

I didn't plan to write a collection of short stories. I wrote the first one, "The Factory," because I needed a break from writing my never-ending doomsday novel series, *The Touchers*.

The break lasted for more than a year and resulted in these fourteen tales, presented here in the order in which I wrote them. The stories cover a wide variety of genres: horror, thriller, ghost, sci-fi, fairy tale, fantasy, and humor. Nearly all have a touch of the supernatural.

Some of the tales have interesting origins:

* "The Factory" stems from my fascination with the many red brick buildings—former mills—you see along Route I-84 in Connecticut and New Hampshire. I've always wondered what it would have been like to work in one of those old factories.

* "Everything $50!" was inspired by a dream in which I was charged fifty dollars just to enter a store. When I woke up, I realized the concept was ridiculous, as many dreams are. But then I thought: *What if there was a store where everything cost fifty dollars?*

* During a long wait in a hair salon, I got an idea for a story—about hair, of course. "The Rapunzel Effect" is the result of that experience.

* A discussion about the importance of language led to "Wordless." It's my take on what might happen if people lost their ability to use words.

* A former coworker has an intriguing job: She waters office plants. Her unusual occupation inspired "The Plant Whisperer."

* While writing this introduction, I read a magazine article about Hello Barbie, a new interactive doll that talks to girls. "Jeremy's Toys" is a tale about toys that talk to a little boy. How ironic!

The fourteen stories were great fun to write; I hope they'll be great fun to read.

STORIES

THE FACTORY

It was an ordinary factory building—the kind you see all over New England—an ugly red brick structure that filled an entire city block. At one time, it had been a booming center of activity with hundreds of workers; now it was just a vacant shell.

Annie Lemieux thought about the factory a lot. She was the receptionist for Handler's Insurance Agency, located directly across the street, and her desk faced the building. In fact, that was all she saw through her window. The factory had looked the same since she took the job, nearly seven years ago.

The city, which now owned the building, had repaired the factory's broken windows and maintained the property, optimistically posting a big "**FOR SALE or RENT**" sign on the front lawn. But the city had been unable to sell or even rent space inside because, through the years, the neighborhood had morphed from an industrial area to a gentrified residential one. Since the factory was no longer zoned for heavy commercial use, it was worthless to nearly all prospective buyers.

But apparently it wasn't worthless to everybody. When Annie came to work one morning, she noticed the old sign had been replaced by a single-word sign: "**SOLD**." She checked her phone to find out the details of the sale, but there was no information on the Internet.

"Does anyone know who bought the factory across the street?" she asked Austin Reemer, one of the insurance agents.

"Not a clue," he said.

At lunchtime, she bought the daily newspaper and checked the articles, finally finding a tiny story on the bottom of page nineteen, which said the city had sold the factory to an "undisclosed buyer" and that it would be used for "storage purposes only."

When she reported this update to her coworkers, two of them chuckled.

"What're they gonna store in there?" Marv Phillips asked. "Dead bodies?"

Lindsey Scott poked him in the back. "Nah," she said. "I bet it'll be used for illegal drugs."

Annie listened but didn't laugh or comment because she didn't think their remarks were funny. She also didn't agree with either of them.

The new owner of the building—whoever it was—moved quickly. The next day, trucks pulled up in front of the factory and Annie watched as bands of workers hauled out old machinery, tossing the pieces into huge dumpsters that lined the whole block.

At lunchtime, Annie stood in front of her office, eating a strawberry ice cream cone, as the men continued to pile factory debris into the giant containers. When she saw bolts of dusty, but still colorful, fabrics thrown away—many with floral and paisley prints—she remembered hearing that the factory had once manufactured women's clothing.

She tried to imagine what the building must have been like then, with men and women working on large looms—or maybe rows of sewing machines—and made up her mind to find out what the inside of the factory had really looked like.

Back at her desk, Annie tried to ignore the activity across the street, but it was difficult because of the constant noise.

"What're they doing over there?" Lindsey asked, covering her ears.

Duh! "They're cleaning out the building," Annie said.

"Yeah, I know that. But why is it so loud?"

Annie thought before replying, trying to figure out how to best explain the situation to the ditz. "They don't have a loading dock in the back anymore," she finally began. The city had removed that industrial eyesore to appease the neighbors.

"So?"

"So now the workers have to take all the machines apart before they can carry them out the front."

"Why?"

"Because they're too big."

"Oh." Lindsey nodded her head as she walked away.

Annie sometimes wondered why the firm had hired Lindsey. But, of course, she knew the answer: Lindsey sold insurance policies; she had movie-star looks.

When Annie arrived at work two days later, the huge container bins were gone, replaced by a line of trucks and vans, the names on the vehicles describing their trades: "Victor's Electric," "Sardoni Plumbing and Heating," "New Century Carpentry," "Mitchell Steele Contractors."

The renovation phase at the factory took longer than the cleanup; the last truck departed after nearly a week.

During that time, the noise was even worse than before, with the buzzing of power drills and pounding of hammers making it difficult for Annie and her coworkers to talk to clients in person or even on the phone. Several agents didn't report to the office at all, saying they were working full-time at home instead. Annie wasn't sure if they were telling the truth or not. But, as the receptionist, she had no choice. She had to stay at her desk and suffer through the noise.

Besides, Annie had no desire to stay home. Although she was thirty-one, she still lived with her widowed mother, a mean-spirited alcoholic, whose greatest pleasure in life was to put down her only child.

Each day, Annie could expect a variety of stinging criticisms from Mom. This morning's farewell taunt had been, "That top makes you look like a horse." Annie was a little overweight and Mom made sure she always remembered it.

Other remarks criticized Annie's looks, intelligence, lack of friends (male and female), choice of job (Annie agreed with that one), and personality. Even with the deafening noise from the factory, being at work was better than spending the day at home with sweet-talking Mom.

The renovation fleet was followed by one more truck—Westfair Pro Painters—whose crew worked quietly. With no more distracting noise, the sensitive-eared agents returned to the insurance office.

For the first two days, the painters worked inside the factory so Annie had no idea what they were doing. But, on the third day, even though the paint crew was still inside, she knew. They were painting the rectangular multi-paned windows: Every window was becoming black.

"Cool," Lindsey said, pointing at the factory. "I like the red and black—kinda scary, like a haunted house in a carnival."

"But why would anyone permanently cover up all the windows?" Annie asked. "No one in there can ever see anything outside."

"True," Austin agreed. "But no one outside can see in there either, and, since it's dead storage space, they probably want to make sure no light gets in." He shrugged. "Hey, it's cheaper than buying shades, especially since no people will be working in the building."

That answer made a lot of sense. But Annie still didn't like the black windows.

After the painters left, nothing seemed to happen in the factory. Each afternoon after lunch, Annie walked around the building, checking to see if she had missed any activity.

She discovered a small back door, which, to Annie's knowledge, had never been used, even by the repairmen. One afternoon, Annie saw a white van parked in the street next to the rear door. Unlike the other vehicles that had been involved in the factory makeover, this van had no name printed on its side. Annie tried to peek through the van's windows, but they were tinted so it was impossible to see anything.

After that, she checked the rear door of the factory every weekday afternoon. One other time, she saw a large unnamed black truck parked nearby. However, like the white van, the truck's windows were tinted and Annie couldn't make out anything inside.

At home, Annie used the Internet to find out more about the factory's history. She discovered the building had first been used to manufacture shoes (Steigler's Shoe Company), then hats (Premier Hat Factory), and finally clothing (Arcadian Fine Ladies' Apparel).

She searched for details about each of the companies and, when she found nothing, used her imagination to fill in the blanks. She pictured rows of huge tables filled with buttoned women's shoes, ornate hats, and long fitted dresses. In the background were looms and sewing machines.

The open floor was noisy and busy, but it was clean and the workers were happy. In fact, the women sewing and weaving, as well as the men and women assembling clothing at the big tables, were all smiling and singing.

Annie realized her picture of the factory was totally unrealistic, but she liked it anyway. *Why not? It's my vision.*

Annie enjoyed her daily lunchtime walks around the factory. It was good exercise too, she reasoned, but she kept feeling she was missing something.

She didn't see any more trucks or vans parked at the building. Although the factory had been sold, from the outside it was still the same ugly red brick building except, of course, for the black painted windows. The **"SOLD"** sign had been removed and nothing indicated the factory's new use.

It's just like before, Annie thought as she began her customary after-lunch walk. But when she reached the back of the building, she noticed a tiny ray of light filtering through the bottom of the rear door. Marching to the entrance, she turned the knob. To her surprise, the door wasn't locked so—very slowly—she pushed it open.

The sound indoors was so loud that Annie was amazed she hadn't heard it outside. And the sunlit room was filled with men and women happily working on looms, sewing machines, and large tables—much like she had imagined.

She held her hand up to her mouth and just stood in the doorway, taking in the impossible scene.

"Miss?" a male voice next to her asked.

Annie turned to see a whiskered man staring at her.

"Can I help you?" he asked.

"I don't understand," she stammered. "I..." Glancing down, she realized she was no longer dressed in a gray striped blouse and black knit pants. She was now wearing pointy buttoned shoes and a long fitted shirtwaist dress in a paisley print—the same pattern she had seen the workers haul out in a bolt weeks ago. In her hands, she clutched a small navy purse, not the black shoulder bag she had been carrying.

"Is something wrong, Miss?" the man continued. "When I saw

you standing here by the open door, I thought you were interested in the assembly job, but..."

Annie quickly made a decision. She looked up at the man and smiled. "Everything is fine," she said. "And I am interested in the job."

"Please follow me," the man said.

Annie entered the factory.

When Annie didn't return to the office after lunch, her coworkers did nothing, figuring she had gotten sick or simply decided to play hooky. The fact that Annie had never left work without notice didn't matter to them; they didn't really care.

However, their boss, Fred Handler, did ask about Annie's whereabouts.

"She had to leave early," Marv Phillips lied, assuming he was covering up for a coworker.

After Annie's mother reported her daughter's disappearance, the police began an investigation. When they learned about Annie's obsession with the factory across the street, the police checked the property and, next to the locked rear door, found her pocketbook— intact with full wallet, keys, and phone. But they found nothing else.

The city police received permission from the building's mysterious owner—which turned out to be the U.S. government— to examine the interior, even though federal officials assured them the building had been locked since the renovation.

In the factory, police found only boxes and files stuffed with papers, placed on the unfurnished floors for storage by an unidentified government agency. There were no fingerprints left by Annie and nothing to indicate she had ever been inside.

The police concluded she had been kidnapped outside the rear door of the factory building. They hunted for her abductor, but with no clues, eventually gave up the search.

Annie Lemieux was never seen again.

EVERYTHING $50!

Kelly Burnside had walked past the block many times and never noticed the store. Yes, it was small. But still she wondered how she had never seen the bright green sign: "EVERYTHING $50!"

Maybe because, until today, I never had fifty dollars, Kelly thought as she stood in front of the store's window. There was just one item displayed, but it was something she really wanted—a Galaxy smartphone.

Kelly had checked the phone's price and it was much more than fifty dollars, and that didn't include monthly charges. But the store's sign said "EVERYTHING $50!" and for her fourteenth birthday last week, her mom had given her money: a crisp new fifty-dollar bill, perfect except for a green dot on President Grant's nose. Slowly, Kelly opened the door and stepped inside the store.

"Good afternoon," a chubby little white-haired lady said, walking over to her. "Can I help you?"

"That phone." Kelly pointed to the window display. "Is it really fifty dollars?"

The saleslady chuckled. "Of course it is, dear. Everything in the store costs fifty dollars."

"But I've checked the price of that phone," Kelly said. "It costs at least one hundred dollars everywhere else."

"Not here," the saleslady said, her dark eyes twinkling. "Would you like to buy it?" She moved to the window and picked up the smartphone.

As Kelly scanned the small shop, she saw very few items on display—just a suitcase, a laptop computer, a coat, and a dress. "You don't have many things in the store," Kelly said when the woman returned.

"We sell closeouts and overstocked items—good products only," the saleslady explained. "No irregulars or factory-repaired models, so often we have just a few things for sale. You never know what you'll find." She handed Kelly the Galaxy phone. "See if this is what you are looking for."

Kelly examined the phone. "It seems good," she said. "But does it work?"

"Of course, dear. And it's fully guaranteed."

"How much are the monthly charges? I don't know if I'll be able to afford them."

The saleslady laughed and waved her hand.

At that moment, Kelly thought the woman looked like someone she knew, but she couldn't think of who it was.

"There are no monthly charges," the saleslady said. "No tax either. Everything is included in the price."

"So it's just fifty dollars?"

"That's what the sign says."

The phone worked fine. Kelly was thrilled with it and she told her mother about her experience.

"It doesn't make sense," Mrs. Burnside said.

"I know," Kelly agreed. "But it did happen and I have my receipt right here." She showed her mother the piece of paper the saleslady had given her. It had the store's name, the price of the smartphone (with all monthly fees included), and the return policy: "Money back within 30 days."

Kelly's mother examined the receipt carefully. "It looks okay," she finally said. "The only thing I don't see is the salesman's name, which is usually on here."

"That's probably because it's such a tiny store and she was the only person there."

"Probably."

"The lady was very nice and she reminded me of someone, but I couldn't figure out who. You might recognize her. It's a great store, Mom, and she said they get new stuff in all the time. Maybe you can go there with me."

Kelly's mother smiled. "Maybe I will," she said.

Since Kelly no longer had fifty dollars, she avoided the little store, afraid she'd see something else she wanted. But on a Friday afternoon, two weeks after her smartphone purchase, Kelly's mother waved a fifty-dollar bill in front of Kelly's face.

"I've saved this so I can go to that store with you, Kel," she said. "I'd like to see what's in there."

"Sure, Mom. Let's go."

Kelly and her mother walked the few blocks to EVERYTHING $50! But when they reached the store, Kelly saw a big white sign on the door and frowned.

"That's strange," Kelly's mother said, looking at her watch. "Why would they be closed now? It's not even five o'clock."

"And it was around five when I bought the phone," Kelly added as she pointed to the window display. "Is this something you'd want to buy?"

Kelly's mother looked at the item in the window and laughed. "I'm sure fifty dollars is a great price for that iron and ironing board. But when did you ever see me iron?"

"Never."

Mrs. Burnside put her arm around Kelly's shoulder. "Come on, Kel. Let's go home."

Kelly probably would have forgotten about EVERYTHING $50! if she hadn't used her smartphone all the time. It reminded her of the little store.

About a month after the disappointing trip to the store with her mother, Kelly got a babysitting job from the people who lived in the apartment across the hall.

"We need you to stay with Freddie and Tina all afternoon next Saturday," Frank Armato explained. "We'll be at a wedding."

"Sure," Kelly said. She liked the Armato kids. Freddie was five and Tina was three and, unlike other kids she babysat, Tina and Freddie usually did what Kelly told them to do.

On Saturday, Kelly played games with the children—they loved hide and seek—and when Tina and Kelly watched a Mickey Mouse movie, which Freddie called "a baby show," the little boy played in his room with cars and trucks.

The Armatos got home just as the kids were finishing their macaroni and cheese dinners.

"I hope it wasn't too much work," Nancy Armato said as she ran to the table and hugged both kids like she hadn't seen them in weeks.

"No, we had lots of fun."

"Here," Frank said, handing Kelly a fifty-dollar bill. "Thanks for helping us out today."

Kelly waited till she was in her room to examine her babysitting money. She plopped onto her bed, took the fifty-dollar bill out of her jeans pocket, and stared at it. There was the picture of President Grant, just like her birthday gift and...

Kelly sat up, not believing what she saw. The president's nose had a big green dot—just like the birthday bill she had used in

EVERYTHING $50! *How could that be?*

When her mother came home, Kelly showed her the fifty-dollar bill. "It must be the same one you gave me," Kelly said, shaking her head. "I don't understand."

"It could just be a coincidence," Mrs. Burnside said. "Maybe the Armatos shopped in that store, paid with a hundred-dollar bill, and got your fifty as change." Kelly's mother shrugged. "Or maybe a bunch of fifties were printed with a green spot on the nose—or someone just marked up a bunch of bills. It could be anything."

Kelly thought her mother's ideas made a lot of sense. But none of them felt right. "I'm going to copy the number that's on here," she said. "Then, if I see another fifty-dollar bill with the green spot, I'll know for sure if it's the same one."

"Sherlock Kelly," her mother said, laughing. "I wonder what you're going to do with your money."

Kelly smiled.

Kelly didn't think EVERYTHING $50! would be open on Sunday, but the next morning, she went there anyway. This time, the window display featured an iPad mini—the exact model Kelly wanted.

There was no "CLOSED" sign so she turned the knob and the door opened.

"Good morning, dear," the chubby lady with the short white hair said. "Can I help you today?"

Kelly glanced around the store and again saw just a few items—a man's briefcase, a big TV, and a framed painting of a soldier riding a horse. "That iPad mini in the window," she said. "It's only fifty dollars?"

"Yes, of course."

"There's nothing wrong with it?"

The woman laughed, her double chin bouncing. "Is there anything wrong with your phone?" she asked.

"No, the phone works great."

The saleslady walked to the window, removed the iPad, and handed it to Kelly. "Here," she said. "Try it out."

Kelly turned on the iPad mini and played with it for several minutes. Then she shut it off.

"It's perfect," Kelly said, giving the saleswoman her fifty-dollar bill.

Kelly loved her iPad mini as much as her smartphone and she didn't think she wanted to buy anything else. Besides, she didn't have fifty dollars.

About a week after Kelly bought the iPad, her mother knocked on Kelly's door. "Mail for you," Mrs. Burnside said, waving a letter.

Kelly grabbed the letter and checked the return address. "It's from Aunt Monica," she said. "What is it?"

Kelly's mother smiled. "You won't know until you open it."

Kelly tore open the envelope and read the first page of a card: "Happy Belated Birthday!"

She turned to her mother. "It's two months after my birthday. I thought Aunt Monica forgot."

Mrs. Burnside shrugged. "So did I. But you know my ditzy sister..."

When Kelly opened the card, a fifty-dollar bill floated to the floor. She picked up the bill and studied it carefully. "It's got the same green spot on the nose. I bet it's the same one." Kelly rushed to her desk and took out a sheet of paper.

"Here." She gave the bill to her mother. "Check the numbers I copied: JL61251807A. Is it a match?"

"Yes," Kelly's mother said. "But Monica lives two thousand miles away so how could she have had that particular fifty-dollar bill?"

"I told you it would be the same one."

"I guess money really does travel fast," Mrs. Burnside said, smiling at her daughter. "I bet I know what you're going to do with this money."

Kelly waited nearly a week before visiting EVERYTHING $50!, mostly because she wasn't sure what she wanted to buy. Then she saw something in the window of a high-priced clothing store and later checked the item online. It cost two hundred dollars. "No way," she whispered.

But Kelly was curious about what she would find in EVERYTHING $50! so, after school, she walked to the store.

This time, the window display was disappointing; it was a large black leather designer handbag. She turned the doorknob and entered the store.

"Hello again, dear," the white-haired saleslady said. "Can I help you today?"

"I'm not sure," Kelly said. "I don't want the pocketbook in the window."

"Maybe you'd like one of these?" The woman pointed to a tan recliner, a cactus plant in a fancy gold pot, and a pair of skis.

"I don't even know how to ski," Kelly said.

"You could learn."

Kelly shook her head. "It costs too much."

The woman nodded and then raised her hand. "Wait a minute," she said. "I just remembered that we got in a small shipment earlier this afternoon."

She returned almost immediately, carrying a pair of skinny jeans—the same designer jeans Kelly had seen in the expensive store. She looked at the label—and, of course, it was her size.

"I don't understand. How...?"

"It just happens," the saleslady interrupted, her eyes twinkling. "Sometimes we're able to find just the right item for our customers." She smiled at Kelly. "Would you like to try on the pants?"

"No, I'm sure they'll fit great."

"I think so too, and, if not, you can always return them for a full refund."

Kelly took out her fifty-dollar bill and gave it to the saleslady.

Kelly loved her new jeans as much as her smartphone and iPad. She thought EVERYTHING $50! was the world's greatest store. She would have told her friends in school about it, but she didn't have any because she was shy with kids her own age and didn't start conversations.

However, when Kelly wore her new jeans to school, Maria complimented her and asked Kelly where she'd bought them. Kelly told her about EVERYTHING $50!

"I'd like to check that store out," Maria said. "Want to go with me today after school?"

"Sure," Kelly replied. She really liked Maria, but had always been too scared to approach her.

The girls walked to EVERYTHING $50! But when they arrived at the store, it was dark and empty. A "FOR RENT" sign covered the locked door.

"I'm so sorry," Kelly said. "I didn't know the store was closed. I was here just last week."

"That's okay. You said they didn't have much for sale anyway and you probably got all the best stuff."

"Yeah," Kelly agreed. "I sure did."

A few months later, Kelly and Maria were best friends who did everything together. Maria had just left Kelly's apartment and, with winter over, Kelly was emptying her sweater drawer. As she stood on a chair, piling bulky sweaters on the top shelf of her closet, she accidentally knocked an old children's book onto the floor. It landed with the front and back covers facing up.

"*Cinderella*," Kelly read as she stepped off the chair to pick up the book. When she flipped it over to the open pages, she immediately recognized the picture: It was a smiling chubby face with twinkling dark eyes and short white hair.

"Oh my God!" Kelly shouted, the book falling from her hands. Cinderella's fairy godmother looked exactly like the saleslady in EVERYTHING $50!

THE WOODS

"We picked the best day for a hike," Lily Montero said, gazing at the blue cloudless sky.

"Yeah," Bryan Erskine agreed. "It's gotta be about seventy degrees—not too hot or cold. Just right."

The couple entered a treed area that everyone called "The Woods." Although it was big enough to be a park, it wasn't town land. In fact, no one seemed to own the secluded strip of greenery, which made it a great place for college kids like Lily and Bryan. They went to The Woods all the time, and not always to hike. It was a perfect hangout for drinking and sex—especially during warm weather.

As they walked, Lily and Bryan carried backpacks filled with food for lunch. They planned to hike a few miles, have a picnic—and then...They hadn't discussed after-lunch plans, but neither of them had classes until late in the afternoon.

The couple walked along a trail made by other hikers, listening to the melodic birdcalls and admiring the stately trees until they reached an open area.

"What a mess!" Lily exclaimed. The site was full of crushed beer cans, dirty napkins, and a large pizza box. "I guess some people can't be bothered with cleaning up their garbage."

"We'll do a better job," Bryan said, putting his arm around Lily's shoulder. "Come on. We're not gonna eat here."

Lily and Bryan hiked further into The Woods, following the well-trampled little path.

"I'm tired and hungry," Lily said when they reached a second clearing. "Let's just stop here."

"Not yet," Bryan said. "We're supposed to be hiking and we haven't even gone two miles."

"Can't we walk more after lunch?"

"Not right after lunch," Bryan said, caressing Lily's face. "I've got other plans."

Lily smiled and kissed him softly on the lips. "So let's just stay here and eat." Then she turned away and spread her hands. "It's nice and clean and real quiet."

Bryan shook his head. "I ate a late breakfast so I'm not hungry yet." Tugging at Lily's hand, he pulled her towards the trail. "We'll just go another half mile and then stop and have lunch. Okay?"

"I guess."

They continued walking through The Woods.

After Lily and Bryan hiked another quarter of a mile, Bryan stopped and stared at the ground.

"What's the matter?" Lily asked.

"Take a look at this." He pointed to a smaller trail jutting from the main path. "I never noticed before, but some people went that way. I wonder what's over there."

"You said we could eat lunch at the next clearing and there's one just around the bend. We can check out this other trail before we go back."

"Come on." Bryan pulled her arm again. "It'll just be a couple more minutes."

They walked for a half-mile surrounded by trees and thick shrubs.

"There's nothing here," Lily complained. "Now I'm really starving and there's no place for us to sit and eat. We have to turn around and go back."

"No. Some people went this way so there's gotta be something here."

"So stubborn," Lily muttered, but she kept walking.

About a half-mile later, Lily and Bryan were forced to stop when a chain-link fence blocked their way. A large sign on the fence read, "**DANGER! DO NOT ENTER!**"

"Oh, great!" Lily whined.

Bryan looked in all directions. "Maybe we can walk around the fence and pick up the trail again," he suggested.

Lily dropped to her knees. "Bry, I'm so tired. Can't we just eat here?"

"There's not even enough room to spread the sheet."

"Fine." She stood up. "Let's go."

They walked another quarter of a mile, but the fence didn't end.

"Give it up," Lily said. "We have to go back to the regular trail. There's nothing here."

"Yeah, I guess you're right."

"I am so damn hungry. We should just sit down right here and eat."

"No." Bryan approached the fence and stuck his finger through one of the links. "See all the open space over there? That's a much better place for us to eat. And inside the fence, no one'll bother us."

"No one else will be on this stupid little trail anyway—and don't forget the big sign that says, 'Danger!' They must have put the fence up for a reason."

Bryan chuckled. "What kind of danger can be in there?

Poisonous plants? Bears? The people who own this land probably just want to keep some of it private for themselves."

"For their own picnics?"

"Maybe. This fence isn't that high. I'll help you climb over."

Lily and Bryan spread their sheet under a majestic tree with floppy oval leaves and gnarly roots, some of them protruding through the grass.

"Maybe we should find a place that's less bumpy," Lily said.

"I thought you were starving?"

"I am."

"Then let's just stay here." Bryan sat on the sheet and smoothed it with his hands. "It's comfortable enough."

Lily nodded as she opened both backpacks to take out their lunches. In addition to two peanut butter and jelly sandwiches, she had packed a large bag of potato chips, a cheese dip, and four drinks—two bottles of water and two sodas.

"Sorry," Lily apologized as she spread their food on the beige sheet. "It's not a real fancy picnic."

"That's okay. I'm still not hungry so you go ahead and eat." Bryan grabbed a bottle of Pepsi and lay on the sheet, watching her.

Lily gobbled her sandwich and dove into the chips.

"Feel any better?" Bryan asked, smiling.

"Much." Lily drank some water and returned his smile.

"If you're still hungry, go ahead and eat my sandwich."

"Are you sure? Thanks." Lily quickly ate half of her boyfriend's lunch. As she rewrapped the rest of the sandwich and shoved it into Brian's backpack, Lily squinted. "What's that?" she asked.

"What?"

"There's something on the ground." Lily walked a few feet from their sheet and picked up a small piece of plastic. "It's a Visa card," she said. "The name on it is Phillip Johnson."

"So we're not the only ones who found this great forbidden

spot."

"Yeah. But why would someone just leave his credit card here? Wouldn't he have come back to look for it when he realized it was lost?" Lily placed the card in her backpack, scooped up her bottle of water, and remained standing.

"He probably didn't figure the card was here or looked and couldn't find it," Bryan said. "Or maybe he didn't even bother to look, cancelled this card, and got a new one."

"Maybe."

Bryan rolled onto his back and gazed at the clear blue sky. "See how nice and peaceful and private it is in here?" he said. "This turned out to be the perfect place for a picnic."

"Yeah, I guess. But I still don't understand that warning sign."

"No matter." He smiled at Lily and opened his arms. "If you're finally finished with lunch and solving mysteries, come over here and join me."

Lily drank another sip of water and smiled at Bryan. She took a step towards his open arms, but then stopped and frowned.

"What's wrong?" Bryan asked.

"Something just moved under the sheet."

"I didn't feel anything. You're just making an excuse not to be with me."

Lily dropped the water bottle and backed away. "No," she said. "I swear. Something moved in the corner, right by the backpacks."

Bryan sat up. "Okay, you got my attention now and I'm watching." He stared at the backpacks for a long moment. "Nothing's moving over there."

"Well, something did before. Maybe it was a mouse..."

"Or a great big bear!" Bryan growled, raising his arms as if he was about to pounce on her.

"That's not funny. I saw something move under the sheet and I'm not going anywhere near there."

"I guess you'll do anything to stay away from me."

"Bry, let's pick up the sheet and get out of here. I'm scared."

"Fi..." He didn't finish the word.

"What?"

"Something just moved under my leg."

"Get up right now!" Lily shrieked.

Bryan stood and took a step toward Lily. As he walked, a large root ripped through the sheet and wound itself tightly around his left foot.

"Get it off!" Lily shouted.

Bryan reached down to pull the root away. "It's not coming off!" he shouted. "Help me!"

As Lily inched closer to the sheet, she saw more movement under the tree. "Bry, there're more roots coming over here," she said.

"Roots can't move fast like this." He tugged harder at the rope-like vegetation, now wrapped around his leg up to the knee. "Do you have a knife?"

"We ate sandwiches, remember?"

A second root burst through the sheet, grasped Bryan's right leg, and slithered slowly up his jeans. He tried to stand, but the two roots yanked him down onto the sheet.

"Lily, I'm stuck!" Bryan, now forced into a sitting position, still attempted to free his bound legs. "I can't move." He looked like he had been lassoed.

As Lily took one step closer to the sheet, another root popped out of the ground and groped for her right foot. She jumped out of its path, backing further away. "I can't get any closer!" she yelled. "The roots won't let me."

While Lily watched, another root tore through the sheet and wrapped itself around Bryan's left arm. Although he tugged on the new root with his remaining arm, it didn't budge.

"Run and get help!" Bryan shouted.

"We're in the middle of The Woods—not even on the trail. There's no one anywhere near here!"

"Just go!"

Lily nodded. As she raced to the fence, she saw another root take hold of Bryan's right arm, pinning him onto the sheet.

"No!"

Lily was a yard from the fence when she heard Brian's terrifying shriek. She turned just as a group of synchronized roots dumped Bryan and their picnic gear into a freshly made hole in front of the tree.

Lily lunged for the fence and climbed on the chain links. But something latched onto her right ankle and threw her on the ground. She sat against the fence and stared at the impossibly long tree root creeping up her leg. As she tried to pull it off, a second root grabbed her left ankle.

Lily reached into her jeans pocket for her phone and lifted it to call 911. But before she was able to press a number, yet another root grasped her right arm, knocking the phone out of her hand and out of her reach.

As the roots dragged her towards the hole in front of the towering tree, Lily closed her eyes and wept.

DOREEN'S WEDDING

Standing by the door of the reception hall's dressing room, Doreen Hammond carefully removed the plastic wrapping that protected her wedding gown. She looked up at the lacy white dress and smiled. Doreen always smiled when she saw her gown because it was so lovely, exactly the dress she had always wanted to wear when she got married, and now she was getting married in...

Doreen glanced at the faux diamond watch on her wrist. "...in thirty-five minutes," she whispered to herself. Then, realizing the time, she frowned. *Where was Marcy?* Her maid of honor was supposed to be here by now to help with the dress and the veil.

Doreen didn't want to wait any longer to put on the gown so she took off her jeans and tee shirt and stepped, feet first, into the silky soft dress. After zipping the back, she stood next to the full-length mirror on the door and studied herself.

Not too shabby. Yes, the make-up was heavier than she usually wore and her unruly dark brown hair was wrapped into an intricate coif, sprayed into submission. But this was her wedding and she was supposed to look movie-starish. Did she resemble a young Elizabeth Taylor? Maybe just a little.

She slipped her feet into the white-dyed satin pumps and turned sideways. Then she twirled like a ballerina and the fully laced dress bottom swayed with her. *I feel like a fairy-tale princess.*

And she was marrying her prince, Jonathan Fleming. They had met in college, fallen in love, and now they were getting married in...

Doreen looked at her watch again. ...less than a half hour. *But where's Marcy?* Her friend was usually super-reliable so why would Marcy be late today?

Doreen sat on the dressing room's stool and considered her next move. She could continue to stay in this little windowless room, admire herself in the mirror, and wait for Marcy, or she could venture outside and see what was happening. Some wedding guests might already be here, sitting on benches in the chapel, waiting for the service to begin.

She took off the satin pumps, which weren't very comfy, and stepped into her sandals. Then Doreen closed the door quietly and tiptoed out of the room. *If anyone asks why I'm wandering around, I'll just tell the truth, that I was getting antsy.*

She walked into the hallway, which was strangely quiet, slowly opened the door of the chapel, and peeked inside.

The altar and the center aisle were filled with the flowers she and Jonathan had ordered—yellow and blue roses, carnations, irises, and hydrangeas—to match the wedding's color scheme. She sniffed and inhaled the delicate fragrance. But, except for the flowers, the room was empty. No people sat in any of the pews.

She closed the door and looked at her wrist again. The wedding was supposed to begin in less than twenty minutes. *Why weren't any guests here?*

Doreen stood in the hallway, hands on hips, trying to figure out what could be wrong. *Traffic? Maybe a tie-up on the highway?*

No. She shook her head. That theory didn't make any sense; the catering hall was centrally located, near several main thoroughfares. That was one of the reasons she and Jonathan had chosen the place. All the highways couldn't be jammed at the same time. At least some guests should have arrived by now.

And what about Aunt Fran and Uncle Harry? They had traveled here from Florida and were staying at a hotel two blocks away. Since Doreen's parents had both died two years ago, Uncle Harry, her closest living male relative, was walking her down the aisle. She and Jonathan had eaten dinner with them last night. They certainly weren't stuck in any traffic jam.

As she wandered through the hallway, wondering what to do next, Doreen reached a door marked "Office" and knocked. "Hello," she said. "Is anyone in there?"

No one answered.

She tried the doorknob, but it didn't open.

Doreen checked her watch again and realized the wedding was scheduled to start in fifteen minutes. She returned to the chapel and opened the door. But the room was still empty.

Doreen leaned against the chapel door and glanced in the opposite direction. *The banquet room?* Maybe one of the waiters could explain what was happening.

She rushed through the corridor and pushed open the banquet room's double doors. The round tables looked lovely. There were eight of them, circling a parquet dance floor, all outfitted with pale yellow tablecloths, topped with plates, silverware, and elaborate yellow and blue floral centerpieces that one lucky guest at each table would take home.

She stepped inside, walked to the nearest table, and picked up a fluted champagne glass. It was inscribed with a linked "D" and "J," a wedding memento for each guest.

Doreen carefully lowered the glass and once again looked at

her watch. The wedding was set to start in ten minutes and she hadn't seen a single person in the catering hall. *Where was everyone?*

Jonathan! He had to be here. Doreen knew it was bad luck to see the groom before the wedding, but this was an emergency. She stepped out of the banquet room and returned to the hallway trying to figure out where Jonathan could be.

Was there a changing room for the men? She didn't know. But he had to be in one of the rooms.

"Jonathan!" she shouted. But all she heard in reply was the echo of her voice.

The bathrooms? Maybe Jonathan or a few of the guests were in there. Doreen lifted her gown and ran to the other end of the hall. She entered the women's restroom and looked around. The sinks and vanity sparkled and the trashcan was empty. The entire room was spotless; it hadn't been used today.

She returned to the corridor, pushed open the door to the men's room, and peeked inside. "Jonathan?" Doreen whispered.

The room was empty.

She closed the bathroom door and looked at her watch. Her wedding was scheduled to begin in five minutes.

Doreen heard a ringing sound coming from somewhere at the other end of the hallway. *It's a phone,* she realized as she rushed toward the noise. *Someone's calling, maybe to explain what's happening.*

The ringing got louder until she reached the place where it seemed to be coming from—one of the unmarked closed doors.

Doreen turned the knob, but the door didn't open. "Please!" she called. "Please let me in!" She banged heavily on the door with both fists.

The phone rang once more and then stopped.

Doreen checked her watch again and saw it was time for her wedding to begin. She slid to the floor, sat down, and started to cry.

❧ ❧

"Why is she crying?" Mia Washburn asked the supervising nurse.

"I think it's my phone," Cathy Guaragno said as she ended the call and tucked the smartphone into her pocket. "Whenever anyone's phone rings near Doreen's bed, the noise seems to upset her." Cathy tenderly stroked the patient's hand and used a tissue to wipe away the tears.

"The poor lady looks so sad," Mia continued.

"She has reason to be," Cathy said. "Since you're going to be caring for Doreen, you should know her story. She's been like this since her car accident."

"You mean in a coma?"

"Yes."

"When did the accident happen?"

"That's the saddest thing. It happened when she was driving to her own wedding."

"Really? The old lady was getting married."

Cathy smiled wistfully as she moved a strand of the patient's white hair away from her closed eye. "That's what makes Doreen's story so tragic. She was a very young woman then." Cathy turned to face Mia. "That car crash happened nearly fifty years ago."

MIRROR IMAGE

Neal Freeman stood in front of his bathroom mirror, taking a quick shave. It was going to be a busy day—three sales calls in the morning alone—and he didn't want to be late.

Neal checked his reflection in the mirror and liked what he saw. "You're a handsome cuss," he whispered, smiling at the young guy with curly brown hair who smiled back at him.

He picked up a comb, raising his arm to work on his hair, and then stopped. The image in the mirror hadn't seemed to move with him simultaneously. Somehow, it seemed a split-second slower. Neal lowered his right hand with the comb and slowly lifted it again. This time, the two Neals moved in unison.

"Imagining things," Neal muttered, shaking his head. "Must be nervous about today." He finished styling his hair and mouthed a goodbye kiss to his reflection. As the Neal in the mirror returned his kiss, he turned off the bathroom light.

After a long, but successful, day, Neal returned to his apartment. He had sold two spots—one to a hot-shot lawyer, who was spending mucho money. *Enough for the new Miata convertible?* Maybe.

Neal microwaved the take-out Chinese food he had grabbed on

his way home, too tired to spend time sitting in a restaurant eating dinner. After devouring the chicken and broccoli, he grabbed the remote and lounged on the couch, just flipping channels, not really watching anything.

Tomorrow would be another busy day. The station had scheduled two afternoon sales calls and he had a couple of other accounts he intended to see in the morning. His mom was afraid he was working too hard, but Neal wanted the big bucks, and this was the fastest way to achieve his goal.

"You've got to slow down," Mom had said.

"Want me to rob a bank for money?" he had teased.

"Neal, please..."

"Too bad we're not rich 'cause then I wouldn't have to work so damn hard."

"You should give yourself time to enjoy life, get a girlfriend."

"Girls like guys with money. When I've got enough cash, I can get any girl I want."

Neal walked to the bathroom, shaking his head. Lately, all their conversations were always the same. *Maybe if Dad hadn't died...*

He took his toothbrush, added toothpaste, and began brushing his teeth, watching himself in the mirror. But Neal's reflection wasn't brushing his teeth; it was frowning at him.

Neal stared at his image, dumbfounded. This time he was sure the face in the mirror hadn't copied him. Now, however, his reflection wore the same puzzled look as Neal.

He shook his head. *Maybe because I'm so tired...*

But he'd been just as tired lots of other times and the face in the mirror had always imitated his movements and expressions. Neal rested his toothbrush on the sink and quickly raised his right arm. The arm in the mirror did the exact same thing.

He lowered the arm and rotated his head. The image in the mirror moved in unison.

"This is crazy," he murmured and the mirror face mouthed his words.

Neal switched off the light, left the bathroom, and went to bed.

The next morning, Neal entered the bathroom apprehensively, even brushing his teeth without looking at the mirror. But then he felt foolish. *Scared of my own reflection?* Cautiously, he raised his head and examined his face. The reflection looked okay.

"Boo!" he whispered.

The mirror mouthed the word.

Neal smiled and took a deep breath. Everything was fine. He figured he must have been more exhausted yesterday than he'd realized. *Maybe Mom was right...*

As he watched, the face in the mirror shook its head. "No," the reflected image mouthed, lips moving silently.

Neal ran out of the bathroom, slamming the door shut.

He didn't know how long he stood leaning against the closed bathroom door, as if that action could somehow block the face in the mirror and keep it from taunting him. "I need a plan," he finally whispered.

Gotta see if it's in any other mirrors. The bathroom mirror was the only one in the apartment. Neal hurried into his suit pants and shirt—not checking his hair—grabbed a jacket and rushed outside, leaving his attaché case on the chair. He wasn't in any condition to see customers.

The nearest restaurant was just two blocks away. Before visiting clients, he usually had breakfast at Angelo's Café.

"Hiya, Neal!" Gina, the waitress, called as he entered the small coffee shop. "You're real early today."

"Yeah," Neal mumbled, sitting at the counter. "I'll just have a cup of coffee. Gonna run to the men's room first."

As the waitress nodded, Neal dashed to the restroom and

stood, face down, in front of the sink. Then, slowly, he lifted his head and stared at the reflection. The image in the mirror looked scared, almost haunted.

Calm down. Neal took a deep breath and exhaled, the face in the mirror copying his actions.

His hair was messy so Neal used his fingers to smooth some of the wayward strands. He lowered his right hand and the face in the mirror did the same.

Neal smiled; his reflection scowled.

He ran out of the bathroom, out of the restaurant, and onto the sidewalk.

See a shrink? Neal pondered the idea as he walked back to his apartment. *No.* He shook his head. The face in the mirror was real; he was sure of it. A psychiatrist wouldn't believe his story anyway— and what if he tried to prove it? Maybe no one else could see the face. Just him.

Never look in a mirror again? That could work. And if he destroyed the mirror in his bathroom and got rid of all the pieces, the apartment would be safe. *Yeah.* Neal smiled and changed direction. He needed to buy a large hammer.

Neal reached Bolts 'n Nails, but the neighborhood hardware store wasn't open yet. He'd forgotten how early it was. He glanced at his watch and realized the shop wouldn't be open for nearly two hours.

Neal looked up and down the block. Nothing else was open. *Angelo's?* He had ordered coffee and run out of the restaurant like a loony bird. Maybe go back, have breakfast, and make an excuse to Gina to explain his behavior. He turned around again.

Neal felt much better after eating breakfast. He had come up with a story about forgetting to make an important call to a client and having to run back to his apartment to get the information.

Gina seemed okay with it. Hell, she probably dealt with wacky customers all the time. Afterwards, he had tried to make small talk with her and thought he sounded all right—not great, but at least not totally weird.

It was hard to act normal because he couldn't stop thinking about the image in the mirror. He kept seeing his own frowning face. Neal checked his watch and saw it was nearly 9:30. If he walked slowly, the hardware store would be open by the time he got there. Looking straight ahead—not at any store windows where he might see his reflection—he headed to Bolts 'n Nails.

Neal smiled as he left the store with his purchase—the biggest hammer they carried. The tool, which weighed a ton, was certainly powerful enough to destroy his bathroom mirror.

"It'll all be over soon," Neal muttered. "No more mirror."

Neal unlocked the door to his apartment, picked up the heavy hammer, and stepped inside. After tossing his jacket on the couch, he headed straight to the bathroom, his eyes focused on the floor. Then, without glancing at his reflection, he lifted the hammer and drove it as hard as he could into the mirror.

The glass shattered and shards flew everywhere, one piece nicking Neal under his right eye. With blood trickling down his cheek, he reached to open the medicine cabinet—closing his eyes to avoid looking at the broken glass. But when he touched the mirror still attached to the cabinet, another jagged piece fell onto his hand, drawing more blood. Neal shook off the piece and pushed open the medicine chest. He gazed inside, grabbed a box of band-aids, and set it on top of the sink.

However, he couldn't avoid looking at a big chuck of broken mirror that had fallen into the basin. His reflection was bloody and scary-looking—like some kind of frightened ghoul. *Me?* Neal questioned silently. And the face in the broken glass nodded.

Neal rushed out of the bathroom, leaving the band-aids on the sink. He stood in the hallway, breathing deeply, with blood dripping from his hand and staining the hardwood floor.

This is crazy. I can't be afraid of my own reflection. It's just me.

But Neal knew it wasn't him at all. It was something else—something evil.

As the blood continued to drip from his left hand, Neal forced himself to return to the bathroom, trying to avoid staring at the pieces of broken mirror on the floor. Thankfully, the large chunks were angled; they reflected Neal's pants, now splattered with blood, and not his face.

He groped around the sink for the band-aids, not looking at any of the mirrored shards in the now bloody basin. Then, clutching the box, he slowly backed out of the room.

In the hallway, Neal exhaled deeply and headed to the kitchen to clean and bandage his wounds. But as he walked, he stepped on something hard. When he glanced down, he saw it was another large chunk of broken mirror that had landed in the hall. And the face in there was shaking its head and smiling.

Neal sat at his small kitchen table attempting to take care of his wounds. However, his hands wouldn't stop shaking. He took another deep breath and prepared to try again.

He had rinsed his bloody face and hands in the kitchen sink and then dried the cuts with a napkin. But the wound on his hand was still trickling blood and this was his third attempt at attaching a band-aid.

Calm down, he ordered himself as he finally managed to secure the bandage onto his arm. Afterwards, he stared at the result. It was crooked, but at least it covered the cut. When he noticed some blood filling the center of the bandage, Neal tore open a second band-aid and stuck it across the first one, forming a crooked cross.

Then, using a new napkin, Neal carefully patted the cut on his face again. He checked the napkin and saw only a slight tinge of pink. *Good.* He wasn't putting a band-aid on his face. No way he was looking into another mirror.

He leaned back in his chair and closed his eyes. *How'm I gonna pick up the mirror pieces without seeing that face?*

Neal stood by the kitchen entrance, holding a small broom and dustpan. He had dragged the garbage can into the hallway so he'd be able to discard the mirror pieces as quickly as possible. *Feels like a minefield.* He took a cautious step towards the bathroom.

Neal planned to glance at the floor and then scoop up the big chunks without really looking at them. Maybe that way he wouldn't see the face. Afterwards, he intended to vacuum the smaller shards and slivers.

The mirror piece he had stepped on was straight ahead. When Neal reached the broken chunk, he used his broom to sweep it into the dustpan. That worked; he didn't notice the face. Keeping the pan at arm's length, he deposited the glass in the garbage can.

Neal smiled as he walked into the bathroom. There were pieces all over the floor so he bent down and, without looking, swept everything within his reach into the dustpan. When it felt full, he carried the pan to the garbage can and emptied it. Then he returned to the bathroom, filled the pan again, and dumped the load in the trashcan.

From the hallway, he could see that the floor was now clean. But he still had to tackle the sink. Neal marched into the bathroom and, from the door, eyed the basin. In the bowl were at least three pieces of mirror, which he'd have to pick up by hand. *Gloves. I need gloves.*

Dropping the broom and dustpan, Neal hurried to the hall closet and found a pair of black leather gloves. After putting them on, he returned to the bathroom sink. Then, staring at the mirrorless cabinet, he reached into the basin, groped for mirror chunks, pulled out one piece, and dumped it in the garbage. He returned, felt the porcelain bowl again, and withdrew two more jagged chunks.

After adding those pieces to the garbage, Neal went back to the bathroom and peered into the sink. Except for some slivers, it was empty. He ran the water, flushing the tiny flecks down the drain. Then he inspected the floor. No sizeable pieces of mirror remained. "It's over," he mumbled as he returned the dustpan, broom, and gloves to the closet and took out the cordless vacuum.

Neal swept the tiled bathroom floor, humming to himself. But as he swung the door to vacuum behind it, a trapped chunk of mirror toppled forward. Neal stared at it, a horrified expression on his face. However, the image in the mirror wasn't upset; it was smiling. And then an arm reached forward...

Neal dropped the vacuum and raced out of the bathroom. He flung open the hall closet and again found his winter gloves. Before losing his nerve, Neal returned to the bathroom and slowly opened the door.

On his knees, eyes focused on the ceiling, he groped the floor for the piece of mirror. When he grasped it, Neal stood, holding the fragment behind his back and away from his body until he reached the garbage can. Then, as if dumping a dead animal, he quickly raised the lid and discarded the mirror piece.

Neal returned to the bathroom and finished vacuuming the floor. Afterwards, he put the vacuum in the closet and sat in the kitchen, exhausted.

I did it. No more mirror. He looked at his watch. It was nearly noon and he hadn't seen any customers. He decided to change his clothes, grab a quick lunch, and then make his two scheduled calls. "Just no bathroom showrooms," he muttered.

The afternoon went surprisingly well. Neal even made a sale, talking an ambitious young physical therapist into trying a series of local spots. "Damn, I'm good," he whispered as he walked to Bella

Ristorante for a leisurely Italian dinner.

Neal finished both his meal and the bottle of Chianti he had treated himself to. He paid the bill, leaving a generous tip, and stood, intending to go home. Just then he realized he had to urinate. Two words—*bathroom* and *mirror*—flashed into his head.

I won't look. Just piss. The urge was really strong as he rushed into the men's room, locked the door, and quickly urinated. He zipped his pants and, without washing his hands, unlocked the door.

"What's your hurry?" a man's voice asked.

The words seemed to have come from above the sink—the location of the mirror he had been avoiding. Neal twisted the knob and tried to open the door. But the door wouldn't open; somehow, it was jammed. As Neal tugged on the door, a hand reached out from behind and held it shut.

"No," the voice said.

"Let me go," Neal begged. "Please."

"No," the voice repeated.

Two tentacle-like arms grabbed Neal and hoisted him into the air. He tried to scream, but no sound came from his mouth. And then there was only blackness...

A man who looked just like Neal Freeman—minus the cuts on his face and hand—walked out of Bella Ristorante, smiling broadly. He stepped into the dark night and took a deep breath, anxious to get started.

The man reached inside Neal's pants pocket, pulled out a wallet, and counted the bills. *Should be enough,* he calculated, smiling again. But it was too late today; all the stores were closed. *Not to worry.* Strutting confidently, he headed towards Neal's house. *I'll get the guns tomorrow.*

THE RAPUNZEL EFFECT

The trouble was all my fault, although I can't really blame myself. I mean, how could I have known what would happen?

Let me start at the beginning. Marla and I were cleaning out Aunt Jessie's cottage, getting rid of her mountains of junk so we could move in. After my great-aunt died in her sleep at age ninety-two, I was amazed to discover that Jessie had left me—just me—the little house. She gave my parents and brother her money, but I got the cottage, I think because she knew how much I loved the place.

Now Marla and I were spending Christmas break tossing Aunt Jessie's stuff into a dumpster. The plan was for both of us to live here for the rest of college, saving our parents more than two years of dorm fees while having the luxury of our own little house. That was the plan. Only there was so much stuff! It seemed like Aunt Jessie had saved everything.

"Look at this," I said, holding up a small black book with frayed yellow pages. "It says 'Spells' on the cover."

"Cool," Marla said, lowering the porcelain owl she had been examining.

I skimmed the wrinkled pages and frowned. "Unfortunately,

that's the only word I can understand. The rest of this book's written in another language—I don't even know what."

"Lemme see." Marla scooted over. "I think it's Latin," she said. "See all the words ending in 'um' and 'us'?"

The pages were mostly empty; each had only a sentence or two of writing. "Here's a real short one," I said, pointing to a page with just four words. "*Valde longa pilus mea.*"

Marla shook her head. "I have no idea what you just said, except for 'longa,' which sounds like 'long' and 'mea,' which's gotta mean 'me.'"

"I hope it's that I'm gonna live a long life."

"It better not be that it's gonna take us a lot longer to clean up this place."

We both laughed and got back to work.

When I woke up the next morning, something felt different. I walked into the bathroom and looked into the mirror. My hair was longer than when I'd gone to sleep—a lot longer.

"Marla," I said, rushing back into the bedroom and standing in front of her sleeping bag.

"Huh?" She rubbed her eyes and opened them.

"Look at me."

"What's wrong, Deb?"

"My hair. Look at my hair."

Marla sat up and stared at me. "It's like six inches longer than yesterday. How'd that happen?"

"The spell—from the book—didn't it have something to do with 'long'?"

"You think...?"

Without waiting for Marla to finish her sentence, I ran into the living room, found the little book—luckily, I hadn't tossed it—and skimmed through the pages until I again found the words I had spoken. "It's the one that starts with 'Valde,' right? I'm not saying the whole thing aloud again."

"Yeah," Marla said, entering the room. "So what're you gonna do?"

"Something I should have done yesterday: find out what it means." I grabbed my phone and typed in the Latin sentence.

It took awhile to get the answer. I didn't get anywhere when I googled the sentence so I translated the individual words—"my hair very long"—and then called the library when it opened. I spelled the words for the reference librarian.

"It means, 'Let my hair grow very long,'" I said, closing the phone.

"Wow!" Marla stared at me. "You think your hair is gonna just keep growing?"

I shrugged. "I don't know." I fingered a few strands of my new longer hair, which now reached several inches below my shoulders. "It's kind of okay like this, but if it keeps getting longer..."

"Then how do we stop it?"

"Maybe there's a chapter at the end about how to break the spells."

Marla and I checked the whole book.

"Every page is the same," I said, when we'd finished. "No chapters."

"Yeah," Marla agreed. "Just all those little sentences, which must be spells, and nothing else."

I put the book on the table. "What should I do now?"

Marla examined my head. "Well, your hair hasn't grown any longer since we got up so maybe it's just a one time thing."

"Nothing happened yesterday either," I pointed out. "My hair grew during the night when I was sleeping."

"So I guess we'll have to see what happens tomorrow morning."

As soon as I woke up, I knew it wasn't good. I could feel that my hair was a lot longer. "Shit!" I yelled, fingering the bottom of my hair, which now reached the base of my back.

"I take it that your hair's still growing," Marla said, without opening her eyes.

"This sucks!" I shouted. "It's gonna be all the way down to the floor soon!"

Marla bounced up and smiled at me. "Hey," she said. "We're forgetting the obvious solution."

"What?"

"I'll show you." She jumped out of her sleeping bag and ran into the kitchen. I heard drawers and cabinet doors slammed open and shut.

"What're you doing?" I called.

"You'll see as soon as I find it."

I heard another drawer yanked open. "Aha!" Marla exclaimed. When she returned to the bedroom, she was smiling and waving a pair of scissors.

I shook my head. "It can't be that simple," I said.

"How do you know? Maybe they didn't have scissors when these spells were made up."

"The book isn't that old."

"But these spells have gotta be ancient."

"I guess it can't hurt to try," I said as Marla began cutting my hair.

"How short do you want it?"

"Cut up to my shoulders—and make it even, just in case your idea works."

Marla did an okay job—not great, but not horrible. Anyway, if the hair didn't grow back, I could always go to a beauty parlor and have it fixed. We spent the day clearing out Aunt Jessie's cluttered closets and I tried to forget about my hair.

When I woke up the next morning, my hair was down to my knees. "I told you cutting it wouldn't work!" I shouted. "It grew even more last night!"

Marla studied me and nodded. "I think you're ready to play Rapunzel," she said. "All you need is a nice big tower and a handsome prin..."

Before she could finish her dumb attempt at humor, I threw the *Us* magazine I'd been reading at her head. "It's not funny!" I hollered. "You wouldn't be saying that if your hair was long like mine!"

"It's not that horrible, Deb. At least it's only the hair on your head. What if it was nose hair that kept growing, or arm and leg hair—or even worse, armpit hair?"

"Gross!" Although I was really angry, I couldn't help giggling at the image that came to mind. "I'd have to join a circus. You're right. I'm so much better off because I can pretend to be a beautiful princess instead of a hairy ape."

I walked into the living room and picked up the little book. "There's gotta be a way to break this crazy spell."

After we couldn't find any information on the Internet, I again called the reference librarian. "Is this for a school project?" she asked.

"No," I said, playing with my hair. "It's personal, just something I'm real interested in."

The librarian promised to check and call back. But when she phoned a half hour later, it was only to apologize. "I'm sorry, but we don't have any books about antidotes for magic spells in our collection."

"Could another library have something?" I asked.

"I guess it's possible."

I asked her to check other libraries, gave her my name and number, and clicked off.

"The librarian said if another library has a book about breaking spells, it would take about a week for me to get it," I told Marla.

"You don't even know if it'll have the answer for your spell."

"At least it's something, but in a week..."

"Yeah," Marla said, nodding. "By then, your hair's gonna be sweeping the floor."

We'd been working inside Aunt Jessie's house since my hair started to grow, but now I had to go out. I'd promised to visit my parents for dinner one night during the week and tonight was the night.

We tried to find the best way to hide my hair.

"Maybe a big bun," Marla suggested.

"It'll have to be very big," I said.

Marla wrapped my hair and pinned it on top of my head. "What do you think?" she asked.

"It's huge and looks awful," I said, undoing the mountains of hair.

"What if we braid the hair first?"

"Okay." I was willing to try anything.

It took forever to braid all my hair. Then Marla arranged it into another bun.

"What do you think now?" she asked as I checked my appearance in the bathroom mirror.

"It looks better and doesn't feel as heavy. Do you think my parents will notice?"

"They may not and, if they do, you can always say you're using a hair extension."

"Why would I want to do that?"

"I don't know. Think of a reason."

"Sure you don't want to come with me?"

"No, thanks. I'll just chill here."

I sighed. "I wish I didn't have to go. Maybe I should just cut my hair again."

"Remember what happened last time? It'll grow much longer tonight."

"Then I guess I won't cut it," I said, shaking my heavy head. "This really sucks."

"Where'd you get all that hair?" my mother asked as soon as I took off my coat. So much for not noticing.

"You know how I've always wanted very long hair," I said. "So I'm playing around with hair extensions."

"But it looks so much like your own hair." My mother touched the bun. "It feels real and the dark brown color is such a perfect match."

"They do a good job with fake hair these days...How's everything?"

"Nothing's new. We just spoke on the phone this morning."

"Yeah, but now it's evening. Something could have changed during the day—like at work." At least we weren't talking about hair anymore.

Mom shrugged. "Same old, same old..." She squeezed my shoulders. "Come inside and tell us what's going on with Aunt Jessie's place."

By the time I returned to the cottage, my head was killing me. "How did those queens with the tons of hair piled high manage to move around?" I asked as Marla helped me unwind the bun.

"I guess they were used to the pain."

I twirled the two braids in my hands. "Should I leave my hair like this when I sleep and see what happens? Maybe it won't grow as much if it's tied up like this."

"You think?"

I shrugged. "No, but I'm so tired and it can't make it any worse."

"Okay," Marla said. "You're the boss of your hair."

"I wish."

I was wrong again. The next morning, it was worse. I found a measuring tape and was able to figure exactly how much my hair had grown from the rubber bands that held the braids. "It's over a foot longer!" I shouted. "Fourteen inches more hair!"

"I guess you're not allowed to tie up your hair," Marla said. "You have to leave it loose when you sleep."

"How'm I supposed to know the damn rules of this spell?" I flung myself onto the floor, face and hair down. "We've got to figure out a way to end this."

"Maybe you should go see a witch?"

"What?" I sat up and stared at Marla.

"You know, a witch—a magic person, someone who knows about spells."

"There are no witches."

"That's not true. There are witches around. They call themselves something else these days, and maybe one of them can figure out how to break your spell."

"And just how do we go about finding a local witch?"

"The way you find everything else. Google it."

Marla was right. Witches were now known as Wiccans, with a religion, Wicca, and they were all over the Internet.

"But it's not like doctors or even priests," I complained. "I mean, there's no listing for a local Wiccan that I can make an appointment with."

"How about this?" Marla said, looking over my shoulder. "Magically Yours, a Wiccan store. Click on it."

I did.

"See?" Marla continued. "It's got healing stones, crystals, tarot readings, candles, incense—and look at that."

I read the line next to her finger: "Ritual and Spell Supplies."

"Oh my God!" I turned to Marla. "Where's this place?"

"Londondale."

"That's a forty-five minute ride."

"Let's see when the store opens." She yanked the phone from my hand and scrolled to the top. "Ten o'clock. If we eat breakfast now, we can get there right when it opens."

"Shouldn't we call first?"

"Then we can't leave here till after ten."

"Okay," I agreed. "We'll just go."

Marla drove and I sat next to her, trying not to sit on my hair, which wasn't easy. "I should have at least put it up in a ponytail," I said.

"You're not supposed to do that. Remember last night?"

"That was when I slept. Maybe it's okay to tie the hair during the day."

"I wouldn't take the chance."

I sighed and thumbed through the book of spells. "You really think the person in this magic store can help me?"

"The description did say they carry spell supplies."

"If my hair keeps growing, how'm I gonna go back to school next week? It's already so damn long that I'm afraid when I walk I'm gonna step on it and trip."

"Think happy thoughts."

"That's easy for you to say. Your hair isn't down on the floor."

Magically Yours was part of a row of small shops. But, when we got to the store, the lights were off, and there was a sign posted on the door.

"I'm sorry," Marla said. "I guess we should have called first. I forgot that stores could be closed this week for vacation." She shook her head. "We came all this way for nothing."

"Maybe it won't be a waste." I walked into the bakery next door. "Excuse me," I said to the old man standing behind the counter. "The magic shop is closed, but I really need to find the owner. Do you know where he or she could be?"

"Nice hair," the man said, smiling. "Never seen hair that long."

"Thanks." I forced myself to return his smile. "The owner?"

"Her name's Rosinda Farquand and she lives over the store. Don't know if she's home now, but the entrance to the second floor is over there." He pointed to the right. "You ever cut your hair?"

"Thank you," I shouted, running out of the bakery without answering his question. As I rushed toward Marla, I stepped on my hair and fell onto the sidewalk, landing on my knees.

"Are you okay?" Marla asked.

"I told you this would happen," I said as I stood up. "Now I've got a big hole in my jeans."

"And your knee's bleeding." Marla reached into her pocket and took out a tissue. "Here. Use this."

"Thanks." I patted my knee, gently wiping off the blood, and then stretched my leg. "It hurts a little, but I can still walk. Come on. It's early and the guy in the bakery said the owner lives upstairs so she could be home now."

"Unless she went away for the week."

"At least I'm trying to be positive." I hobbled to the door leading upstairs and we climbed to the second floor, with me limping the entire way.

"That really hurt," I complained when we got there.

"I thought you were being positive."

"You try walking up a flight of stairs with a bloody knee and hair sweeping the floor."

"That's why we're here. What's the owner's name?" Both sides of the hallway contained apartments.

"It's a strange name, Rosinda something."

Marla moved from door to door. "Here it is. Rosinda Farquand. Cross your fingers," she said, ringing the bell.

"What d'ya want?" a woman's voice behind the door asked.

"She's home," I whispered.

"Yeah, but she doesn't sound like she wants any visitors."

"Shh." I touched Marla's arm. "Hi," I said, cheerfully. "We came to your store this morning because I really need your help."

"Didn't ya read the sign? Store's closed this week."

"I know, but please, I need you to help me. I drove a long way just to see you."

I heard movement, the knob turned, and the door opened slightly. A messy blonde, who looked to be about fifty, peeked through the chain with bloodshot blue eyes.

"Your hair," she said, laughing. "What the hell happened to your hair?"

"That's why I need your help." I held up the little book of spells. "I found this, read a sentence out loud, and now my hair won't stop growing."

Still laughing, she opened the door. "That's the funniest thing I heard in ages! Come on in."

I don't know what I expected a witch's apartment to look like, but Rosinda Farquand's home was kind of strange. It was dark, with heavy green velvet curtains covering the windows. The living room was bare, except for two huge green velvet armchairs and a long wooden table, which was filled with candles and stones.

"Sit down," the woman said, pointing to the bulky chairs. She was wearing a pink bathrobe and fuzzy pink slippers. "You girls want something to drink?"

"No, thanks," I said, lifting my hair, and taking a seat. The cushion was uncomfortably hard.

Marla shook her head and sat in the other chair.

"Lemme see that book," the witch demanded, reaching for it. Her nails were disappointingly ordinary, not long and sharp. They weren't even polished.

She skimmed through the pages, grunting a couple of times before closing the book. "Where'd you get this?" she asked.

"My great-aunt just died and it was in her cottage."

"Was she a witch?"

"I don't think so."

The woman smiled and nodded. "I bet she was and you didn't even know. Lots of people hide it." She let out a huge laugh. "But not me. I'm proud of who I am."

"Do you have something that can break the spell?" I asked quietly.

"Maybe."

After Rosinda got dressed (a pair of jeans and a black sweatshirt, nothing especially witchy), she took Marla and me into her store. Magically Yours was dark and smelled like incense and candles, which wasn't surprising because the place was packed with both.

The shop was tiny, but there were shelves and counters everywhere. Besides candles and incense sticks, I saw stones, charms, and tarot cards. But there were also shelves filled with books and Rosinda walked to one shelf labeled "Magic Spells."

"Where's the spell you cast?" Rosinda asked, again reaching for my little book.

"Page fourteen," I said. By now I knew the page number.

"This one?" She pointed to those four terrible words: *Valde longa pilus mea.*

"Yes."

Keeping the *Spells* book open, the witch scanned the top shelf and picked up a large unmarked volume. After checking the back index, she turned to a page and looked at it. "Just as I figured," she said, closing the big book and taking my book of spells to the front counter.

"What do I have to do?" I asked.

"You'll see." Reaching under the glass in the counter display,

Rosinda removed a small mirror. "This oughta do it. Here." She shoved the mirror into my hand. "You cast the spell so you gotta be the one to end it."

"How?"

"You just say the words backwards—reading them from the mirror."

"That's it?"

The witch nodded. "Lotta spells get broken this way. It's kinda the universal spell ender."

"Go on," Marla urged. "Just say it."

I looked at the words through the mirror, but it was hard to figure them out. "Can't I just write the words backwards and forget the mirror part?" I asked.

"The words won't work without the mirror," Rosinda said. "But you can write them down first and hold the mirror when you read them."

She gave me a pen and I wrote, "*aem sulip agnol edlaV*." Then, positioning the mirror next the backwards words, I said them aloud.

"What now?" I said, shaking my head. "My hair's still long."

"Your hair grew when you slept, right?"

"Yeah."

"So you gotta wait till tomorrow morning."

"It'll just fall off then?"

Rosinda laughed. "No, it's magic. Your hair'll just disappear."

"All of it? I'll be bald?"

The witch roared, laughing so hard that her eyes watered and she had to sit down.

"You wouldn't think it was so funny if it was your hair," I said, frowning.

"Sorry." She wiped her tears with the back of her hand. "You won't be bald. Only the new hair from the spell's gonna vanish. Your hair'll look just like it did before."

"You're sure about that?"

She nodded. "Don't worry. It'll work."

"Okay, then." I felt dumb. "How much do I owe you?"

"No money." Rosinda waved her hands. "Just give me your aunt's book. As you found out, it's kinda dangerous unless you know what you're doing."

"Gladly," I said. "I sure don't want it."

Marla and I shook hands with the witch and the two of us drove back to Aunt Jessie's cottage.

That night, I went to sleep with hair down on the floor and when I woke up the next morning, my hair was a couple of inches above my shoulders. I checked the pillow and sleeping bag, but, as Rosinda promised, the long hair had just disappeared.

"Like it never happened," Marla said.

"Yeah," I agreed. "Except for all the aggravation."

Five days later, I picked up the book my librarian had found on breaking magic spells and, when I got back to the cottage, thumbed through it.

"Hey," I said to Marla. "The book's got an antidote for the 'Rapunzel Curse.'"

"Reading the words backwards through a mirror?"

"No. 'A true love's kiss.'"

"Maybe you should write to the author."

"I think I'll just return the book. I'm finished with magic."

Unfortunately, I was wrong about that. The following spring, I found a long cylindrical sorcerer's hat wedged in the back of Aunt Jessie's closet. But that's another story.

21 CEDAR LANE

"This is the last one," Melanie Feldman said as she handed the carton to her husband, Richard.

"Thank God," he said. "I can hardly walk anymore."

"How could we have accumulated so much stuff?" Melanie asked as she followed him through the side entrance of 21 Cedar Lane that led to their ground-floor apartment. "We've only been married since May."

Richard dumped the box on the floor of their living room, next to dozens of other filled cartons. "I don't know about you, but I come from a long line of pack rats. Still, I'm not taking all the blame." He pointed to several boxes in the corner. "The ones over there, that you marked in red, aren't mine."

Melanie shook her head. "I know. I save way too much junk. But now that we've got our own big place, I promise I'll be better and throw things away. C'mon." She ran to Richard and gave him a quick hug. "Let's start unpacking."

Melanie and Richard went to sleep early, exhausted from having spent the day moving into the house and unpacking. But, during the night, Melanie heard a tapping noise that seemed to be coming from the living room. She opened her eyes and looked at Richard, but he was fast asleep, snoring lightly.

Stepping into her slippers, she padded into the surprisingly bright living room. The pole lamp was on, illuminating the many cartons that still cluttered the floor. *Did we forget to turn off the light?* As Melanie flicked the switch, she caught a glimpse of something moving in the far corner of the room. It was large and grayish, like a person's shadow.

Melanie stood in the dark for a moment, holding her breath. When she didn't hear or see anything else, she turned on the light and wriggled around the cartons to the spot where she had seen movement. But the corner held nothing but boxes. *Must have been my shadow.* She switched off the lamp and went back to bed.

"I woke up in the middle of the night," Melanie told Richard the next morning during breakfast.

"Why? Were you nervous about being in a new house?"

"Not at all," Melanie said. "I thought I heard someone in the living room."

Her husband lowered his coffee cup and stared at her. "What made you think that?"

"It sounded like a hand knocking on the wall."

"And?"

"And when I checked, the lamp was on. Didn't we turn it off?"

"I guess not. We were so exhausted that we must've forgotten."

"Then I thought I saw something move."

"What?"

"A person's shadow."

"Mel, you must've really been tired. It was windy last night so what you saw and heard was probably a tree branch hitting against the house. I'll have to ask Mrs. Corvin to trim them. Speaking of our new landlady...Here." He handed Melanie a paper plate full of corn muffins. "Try one of Mrs. Corvin's homemade treats."

Melanie chose a muffin and took a bite. "This is delicious. We're so lucky to have her living upstairs."

"Yeah." Richard agreed. "Lots of landlords are bad news."

That evening, after unpacking more cartons, Melanie and Richard were cuddling together on the couch, watching *Law & Order*, when Melanie let out a loud yawn.

"What's wrong, hon?"

"Long day at the hospital. So many patients to exercise that I hardly had a chance to sit."

Richard grabbed his wife's arm and pulled her up. "Time for bed."

Melanie didn't resist. "I hope I sleep better tonight," she said.

"You will."

She fell asleep almost immediately. Sometime during the night however, Melanie felt a cool breeze blowing on her face. Although she turned her head and tried to snuggle under the covers, the wind grew stronger, forcing strands of hair against her cheeks.

Must've forgotten to close a window. As Melanie sat up and opened her eyes, she saw a skinny white-haired woman step through the wall.

"What?" she gasped in amazement, reaching for her still sleeping husband. "Rich...," she started to say and then stopped. *Why wake Richard? What do I tell him — that I saw a ghost?*

Melanie lay down again, shaking her head. *I don't believe in ghosts.* But something strange was going on. *First the knocking and now this.*

She forced herself to close her eyes and, after a while, managed to fall asleep.

In the morning, Melanie told Richard what she had seen.

"You were just so overtired," he said. "That's why you thought you saw someone go through the wall."

"But what about the strong wind blowing on me? The window wasn't open. It's like she wanted me to wake up."

"Mel, you must've had a dream and imagined the woman. There's no such thing as ghosts."

"I know, but I felt a breeze and then I saw..."

"Try to rest a little between patients today and then, I promise, nothing will happen tonight." He kissed his wife and caressed her face. "Now, repeat after me, 'There's no such thing as ghosts.'"

"There's no such thing as ghosts," Melanie whispered.

"Wake up, dear."

The voice whispering in Melanie's ear wasn't Richard's. It was feminine and not at all threatening. Melanie turned toward the sound and slowly opened her eyes. The figure standing by her bed was the same thin elderly woman she had seen slip through the wall the night before.

"Who are you?" Melanie asked as she sat up. There was a strange woman in her home, but somehow she wasn't frightened.

"Shh." The woman put her index finger to her lips and walked out of the room, waving to Melanie to come with her.

Melanie stood and followed, not even bothering with slippers.

"What do you want?" Melanie asked when she reached the living room. "Who are you and how did you get in here? If you don't tell me, I'm calling the police."

"You're in great danger," the woman said. "Please, you've got to listen to me."

"Are you even real?" Melanie put her hand out to touch the woman's arm and felt—nothing. "Richard!" she shouted.

Her husband rushed into the room. "What's wrong?" he asked.

Melanie looked at him, not sure what to say. She was standing barefoot in the living room, all by herself.

"Mel, what's going on?"

Melanie continued to stand quietly, trying to think of an appropriate response. She didn't want to lie to her husband, but...

"I thought I heard something again," she finally said.

Richard shook his head. "I'm sorry you're still so stressed out. I'd hoped you'd sleep better tonight." He put his arm around her shoulder. "C'mon. Let's go back to bed."

"Who lived here before us?" Melanie asked Richard during dinner the following evening. She tried to sound casual, although the question had been floating around her head all day. She was sure the woman ghost had something to do with the house.

"I think Mrs. Corvin said it was her mother. She had the downstairs redone into an apartment so her mother could move in here."

"What happened to her mother?"

"She died."

"Oh, do you know when she died and what she died of?"

Richard stopped cutting his salmon and lowered his fork. "Why all the questions?"

"I'm just curious. You know I haven't been sleeping well so I've had lots of time to think."

Richard took a bite of fish and shook his head. "Thinking about our landlady's dead mother isn't going to help you sleep. Maybe you should read a book at night."

"Okay," Melanie agreed, smiling. "I'll try that."

Melanie still didn't have much free time at work so, during lunch, she gobbled her sandwich and devoted the rest of her break to finding out more of the history of the house at 21 Cedar Lane. Using her phone, she googled the address and got Elaine Corvin as the owner. Then she googled "Elaine Corvin" and got her landlady's age, 54, her address—which, of course, she already knew—and nothing else. When she typed in "mother of Elaine Corvin," she got no results.

That night, as she and Richard went to bed, Melanie placed a spy novel—*Cloaks & Daggers*—on her night table.

"So you are going to try to read," Richard said, smiling as he reached for his wife.

"Just like you suggested. See, I listen to your words of wisdom."

He kissed her tenderly and Melanie knew he wanted more. "I'm sorry, honey, but I'm so very tired," she said, rolling away.

It's only a little lie. But she couldn't make love to him with someone else in the apartment—even if it was a ghost. "I'll just read for a couple of minutes."

Richard grunted and turned onto his side.

Melanie opened the book and began to read, this time hoping for company.

Melanie had read only three pages when she again felt a cool breeze. She looked up and saw the same older woman smiling and signaling for her to follow.

"I need to know who you are," Melanie demanded when she entered the living room.

"That's not important."

"Are you Elaine Corvin's mother?"

The woman stopped smiling and stared at Melanie. "Yes."

"What's your name? Or maybe the question should be what was your name? You're not alive, are you?" *I can't believe I just said that.*

The thin woman shook her head. "This isn't about me," she said. "It's about you and your husband. But you're stubborn so I'll give you the answers you insist on having. My name is Gertrude Engle and, you're right, I'm no longer alive."

"You used to live here."

"Yes."

"Okay, then please tell me why you're here now and what's so imp..."

"Mel! Where are you?"

The sound of Richard's frightened voice ended Melanie's question. Seconds later, her husband entered the living room.

"What are you doing here in the middle of the night all by yourself?" he asked.

"I'm not sure," Melanie lied. "You think maybe I was sleepwalking?"

Now that Melanie knew the name of her landlady's mother, at lunch the next day, she googled "Gertrude Engle." The name was fairly common, with numerous listings. But when Melanie added the word, "obituary," she got the information she wanted: "Gertrude Engle, nee Rosner, 79, died suddenly on August 18 of an apparent heart attack. She is survived by her daughter, Elaine Corvin..."

The article went on to mention the woman's achievements—she had been an elementary school teacher and an accomplished pianist—but none of that seemed important to Melanie. It was the phrase "apparent heart attack" that mattered. Was it really a heart attack that had killed the woman?

I'll ask Mrs. Corvin, she decided, tossing the phone into her bag.

Melanie had no complaints about the landlady. Elaine Corvin had been great to both of them—friendly, without interfering. She had baked those tasty muffins when they first moved in and told them to call her, or knock on her door, if they ever needed anything.

Now Melanie needed something—information. When she got home—an hour before Richard—she climbed the front steps and rang Mrs. Corvin's bell.

"Hi," the landlady said, smiling at Melanie. She was an attractive honey blonde, who would have been stunning if her eyes had been larger. Melanie thought they looked like brown pinholes. "Is anything wrong?" the woman asked.

"No, everything's fine. I just wanted to tell you how wonderful it is living here."

"I'm so glad you feel that way." The landlady opened the door. "Would you like to come in?"

"Thanks, maybe some other time. I just had a quick question. I'm curious about who lived in the apartment before us. Richard said it was your mother."

"Yes."

"And she passed away?"

"Three months ago."

"I'm so sorry. Had she been ill?"

"No, it happened very quickly. She had a heart attack." The woman studied Melanie's face. "But why are you asking all these questions about my mother?"

"Oh..." Melanie thought quickly. "I found an old sweater that may have belonged to her and it got me thinking. I'm sorry if I upset you." She turned and ran down the steps.

Melanie kissed Richard good night and again reached for *Cloaks & Daggers* on her night table. She read an additional five pages before she felt a gentle breeze ruffle her hair.

Melanie jumped a little, but wasn't frightened. There was nothing scary about Gertrude the ghost.

"Can I call you Gertrude?" Melanie asked when they were alone in the living room.

"Of course, dear."

"You died of a heart attack?"

"Yes, but please let me talk."

Melanie nodded.

"My daughter—your landlady—is dangerous," Gertrude continued. "You must be very careful of her." The ghost sighed. "Really, it would be best if you and your husband moved out."

"But why? What did she do?"

Gertrude walked to the couch. "My daughter is a murderer."

"Your daughter killed you?" Melanie's asked, her eyes widening. The ghost nodded.

"Oh my God," Melanie whispered.

Gertrude shook her head. "But I'm not her only victim. Elaine murdered her husband too."

Melanie stood completely still, not saying anything. "Are you sure?" she finally asked.

"Yes."

"But why?"

"Bob had taken out a large life insurance policy—at least a half-million." Gertrude shook her head again. "Elaine always loved money."

"But the coroner and the police...?"

"They didn't suspect anything," Gertrude said. "She poisoned us with a wild plant root that made it look like we both died naturally."

"When did she kill her husband?"

"About three years ago."

"But why did she kill you too? I don't understand..."

Gertrude lowered herself onto the couch, but since she didn't weigh anything, her body didn't dent the cushion. "A few months ago, I was searching her desk for a stamp and I came across pages describing types of undetectable poisons and places that sold them. When I asked Elaine about the list, she got nervous and made up a story about needing poison to kill a mouse. But I didn't believe her. She'd never mentioned anything about a mouse problem—and you don't use exotic, untraceable poisons to get rid of mice.

"That's when I decided to check Bob's death because it had been so unexpected and he'd never had any heart problems. After I found out that aconite poisoning is hard to detect because it looks like a heart attack, I confronted her and, when I threatened to go to the police, she finally admitted it."

"How long after confessing did she kill you?" Melanie asked.

"Two days."

Melanie sat next to Gertrude and stared at her. "You already knew about the poison so how'd she do it?"

"I had a nasty cold and she made me chicken soup." Gertrude shrugged. "I guess I should've suspected, but I didn't. Maybe I just didn't want to. I took a sip and then everything happened so fast. My lips, tongue, and throat started burning and I couldn't speak. I couldn't see clearly and things turned green and yellow—all the symptoms of aconite poison."

"You'd told her you were going to tell the police," Melanie pointed out.

"Yes, but after she started crying, she said it was a horrible mistake and begged me not to turn her in so I told her I would think about it."

"And two days later, she poisoned you."

Gertrude nodded.

Melanie reached for the ghost's hand, but she touched only air, her fingers slipping through Gertrude's diaphanous body. "I'm going to get the police to investigate," Melanie promised.

"Just make sure you don't eat or drink anything Elaine gives you," Gertrude warned.

"I won't," Melanie said as she returned to the bedroom.

At work the next day, Melanie had trouble concentrating on her patients' rehab needs as she tried to figure out a way to convince the police to check Gertrude's story. *How?* she kept asking herself. In mid-afternoon, she finally came up with an idea.

When Melanie got home, she typed a Word document on the computer and printed it. After rereading the paper, she folded it, put it into her pocketbook, and prepared dinner, determined to spend some quality time with Richard.

Poor sweetie deserves it. Been avoiding him and tonight won't be any different. Melanie knew she'd have to lie to her husband once again because, for her plan to succeed, she needed Gertrude's help.

As she lay in bed reading the novel, Melanie wondered if Gertrude would even appear. After all, she hadn't asked the ghost to visit. *Ask a ghost to visit,* she thought and let out a giggle.

"What's so funny?" Richard mumbled.

"Something I just read," Melanie lied.

"Spies are funny?"

"Not really. But Trevor Simpson said something that made me laugh." *Hope he doesn't ask what the spy said.*

Richard didn't and Melanie read for a while, actually getting involved in the story, until she felt a burst of cool air on her left arm. When she glanced up, Gertrude stood by the bed, smiling.

After blowing a kiss to her sleeping husband, Melanie grabbed her handbag and tiptoed into the living room.

"Is it too soon?" Gertrude asked. "Did you talk to the police?"

"Not yet, but I had an idea." Melanie reached into her bag, withdrew the paper she had typed, and placed it on the cocktail table. "Look at this," she said.

When she finished reading, Gertrude turned to Melanie. "Do you think this will work?"

Melanie shrugged. "I don't know, but it's worth a try." She took a pen from her handbag and offered it to Gertrude. "I'll need your signature before I go to the police. Can you still write?"

"I'm not sure. I'm not even sure I can hold the pen."

"Maybe I can help you." Melanie wrapped Gertrude's transparent fingers around the pen and held on. "Try to write now," she said.

With Melanie guiding Gertrude's hand, the ghost was able to sign her name on the bottom of the paper. "Does my writing show?" Gertrude asked.

"Yes," Melanie said. "I can see your name."

The next day, instead of going directly home after work, Melanie drove to the local police station. "I need some help," she told the burly man behind the counter—Officer J. Hughes, according to his nametag.

"What can I help you with?"

Melanie dug into her pocketbook and took out a folded sheet of paper. "My husband and I just moved into a house and, yesterday, I found this note wedged in the back of the linen closet."

Officer Hughes scanned the paper. "Do you know who Gertrude Engle is?"

"She used to live in our apartment. Her daughter, our landlady, lives upstairs."

The policeman glanced at the sheet again. "That's Elaine Corvin?"

"Yes."

"Where's Mrs. Engle? I'd like an officer to talk to her about this."

"But that's the problem," Melanie said. "Gertrude Engle is dead—and she died suddenly, of a heart attack, just like she wrote about Robert Corvin in this paper."

Officer Hughes studied Melanie's face. "You think the Corvin woman poisoned her husband and then her own mother?"

"I don't know," Melanie said, shrugging. "But, after reading this note, I think someone should investigate. Don't you?"

At work the next day, Melanie kept wondering if the police had followed up on her letter. She stopped at Acme Market to buy tilapia filets and fresh asparagus for dinner so, when she unlocked the door, Richard, an accountant for Payne & Finch, was already home.

"Hi, hon," he said, kissing his wife tenderly on the cheek. "How's everything?"

"Fine." She handed Richard the bag of groceries and gave him a hug. "I'll start making dinner."

"Great," Richard said, stepping into the kitchen. "And we've got a special dessert tonight. Mrs. Corvin made us an apple pie. When she came down here, she told me she decided to bake a pie for herself and figured she might as well make one for us too. She's some landlady, isn't she?"

Melanie looked at the pie on the counter and nodded. "Yes," she agreed. "Mrs. Corvin is quite a landlady." Melanie knew she had to explain. "Richard," she began. "We can't eat that pie."

"Huh?" Her husband stared at her, dumbfounded. "What's wrong with it?"

"I don't know. But, today, I found out something scary about Mrs. Corvin."

"What are you talking about?"

"I found a letter written by Mrs. Corvin's mother, you know, the woman who lived here before us."

"Let me see the letter." Richard held out his right hand, palm up.

"I'm sorry," Melanie said, shaking her head. "I don't have the letter anymore. I gave it to the police."

"The police!" Richard grabbed Melanie's arm, propelled her to the kitchen chair, and sat her down. "I want to hear everything. What's going on?"

Melanie told him the contents of the letter. In fact, she told him everything—except her conversations with Mrs. Corvin's dead mother. She didn't think he'd believe that part.

"Why didn't you tell me about all this?" Richard asked after Melanie had finished.

"I'm sorry. I guess I wanted to surprise you with my great crime-solving skills."

Richard fell to his knees and grabbed her arms. "We're partners, remember? You can't do things like play detective without me. Promise."

Melanie nodded.

"You think this pie's poisoned? Even if the stuff in the letter is true—and we don't know that because Mrs. Corvin's mother could have had Alzheimer's or just a crazy imagination—why would our landlady want to kill us? We haven't done anything to her."

"Even so, the police should check this pie. And I don't think Mrs. Corvin's mother—her name was Gertrude Engle—was crazy."

"How would you know?"

Melanie shrugged. "Just a strong gut feeling."

After dinner, Melanie and Richard took the pie to the police station. Officer Hughes, still on duty, told them it would take several days for the test results.

That night, Melanie told Gertrude about the pie and her talk with Richard. "Of course, I didn't tell him about you," she added. "But since he knows everything else, I don't want to keep you a secret anymore so I'd like to wake him now and introduce you."

Gertrude shook her head. "I'm sorry, dear. I'd love to meet your husband, but I can't because he won't be able to see or hear me."

"Why not? I can see and hear you fine."

"I don't understand how all this works. I just know that you're the only person who can see and hear me."

Melanie slid onto the couch as she digested Gertrude's words. "So if Richard comes in now, he'll think I'm crazy, just sitting here and talking to myself."

"But the police have the information about Elaine," Gertrude pointed out. "They should be able to find the poison."

"Especially if it's in the pie," Melanie added.

The phone call came three days later. "The test results were negative," Officer Hughes told Melanie.

"No poison?"

"Nothing but fresh apple pie."

"You're still checking for signs of aconite poison in Elaine Corvin's husband and mother? Right?"

"Yes," the policeman said. "But I don't know the status of that. It may be a while before we know anything."

"Can't they just dig up the bodies and run the tests?"

"We need a court order first."

"How long does that take?"

"At least a week, maybe more."

Melanie frowned as she hung up the phone.

Melanie had just arrived home from work the following day when she heard a knock on the door. Through the glass, she saw Mrs. Corvin holding a pie in her hands.

"Hi," the landlady said, smiling, when Melanie opened the door. "I brought you another pie. I hope you both like blueberry."

"I love blueberry," Melanie said. "But Richard and I are trying to lose weight." She hesitated. "Maybe you want to give the pie to someone else?"

"Don't be silly." Mrs. Corvin strolled through the hallway, into the kitchen, and placed the pie on the counter. "You're both so thin. A little pie won't hurt you if you eat a small piece each night. This is fresh so it'll last for days."

"Thank you," Melanie said.

"My pleasure." Smiling again, the landlady walked out of the apartment.

Melanie showed Richard the pie before they tossed it into the kitchen garbage can. "Why is she doing this?" Melanie asked.

"Maybe she just likes us."

"Richard!" Melanie shouted. "The woman's a murderer! She's already killed two people!"

"We don't know that for sure. The other pie she gave us was fine. There's no proof the letter you found is valid and, most of all, Mrs. Corvin has no reason to hurt us."

"I hope you're right. But it's creepy with her living upstairs and giving us pies all the time. Maybe we should move."

"This is a great apartment—and we just moved in. If Mrs.

85

Corvin comes here with another pie, just take it, smile, and thank her. Don't make a big deal. Okay?"

"Okay," Melanie whispered.

Richard and Melanie were loading their dinner plates into the dishwasher when they heard a knock on the door.

Melanie rushed to the entrance. "It's Mrs. Corvin again," she called to Richard. "What should I do?"

"She knows we're here so go ahead and open the door."

Melanie unlocked the door and faced the landlady.

"Good evening," the woman said, smiling. "I hope I didn't interrupt your dinner."

"No." Melanie nodded towards the kitchen. "We were just cleaning up."

"Did you enjoy the blueberry pie?"

"Thank you. It was delicious."

Richard joined Melanie at the door. When no one spoke, the silence became awkward. "Would you like to come in?" Richard finally asked.

"Yes, I would," Elaine Corvin replied, stepping into the hallway. "I have something I need to discuss with both of you."

Richard gestured to the couch, but the landlady shook her head. "No, thanks. I'll just stand."

Melanie and Richard stood together, facing the woman as they waited for her to speak.

"You lied," Mrs. Corvin began. "I know you didn't eat my pie. If I open the pail, I'm sure I'll find it in there."

"But..." Melanie began.

"Shut up," the landlady ordered, scowling angrily. "I've got a lot more to say."

Richard moved towards the woman. "You can't talk to my wife like that. I think you'd better leave now."

"That's not happening," Mrs. Corvin said, reaching into the

pocket of her jeans and extracting a small pistol, which she waved at Melanie and Richard. "You two sit on the couch and then I'm going to ask questions and you're going to answer them."

Melanie and Richard sat closely together, holding hands, as they waited for Mrs. Corvin to speak.

"Don't try to be a hero," the woman warned, glancing from one to the other. "If either of you makes a sudden move, I'll shoot. Understand?"

"Yes," Melanie whispered.

Richard just nodded.

"Good." The landlady sat in an armchair facing the couple and turned to Melanie. "I heard what you said about me—that I'm a murderer. Why did you say that?"

Melanie hesitated.

"Tell her about the letter," Richard said.

"What letter?"

"I found a letter your mother wrote," Melanie began.

"Where did you find it?"

"In the linen closet."

"Bullshit!" Elaine Corvin stood and approached Melanie. "That's not possible. The closet was cleaned out—nothing was left in there."

"The letter was wedged into the back with just a little piece showing."

The woman returned to the chair and sat again. "And what did this letter say?"

"That you killed your husband for his life insurance policy—that you poisoned him with aconite to make it look like a heart attack."

Elaine Corvin stared at Melanie, frowning. "You said I killed two people. Who else?"

"Your mother also died suddenly from a heart attack."

"And you think I poisoned her too?"

Melanie said nothing.

Mrs. Corvin continued to study the younger woman. "Where's this letter you supposedly found?" she asked.

Again Melanie didn't reply

"Answer the question!" the landlady shouted. Moving closer, she aimed the pistol at Melanie's chest.

"I gave the letter to the police," she whispered.

Elaine Corvin nodded, her beady dark eyes still glaring at Melanie. "That's unfortunate," she said. "For me, but also for you."

The landlady kept the gun pointed at Melanie and Richard, but didn't speak.

"So what are you going to do?" Melanie finally asked.

"I'm going to get rid of you. The problem is how."

"You're poisoning us?"

"No. That won't work any more."

"But if you kill us, the police'll figure you did it," Melanie continued.

"That's enough, Mel," Richard warned. "You're not helping things."

Mrs. Corvin smiled. "That's okay. It really doesn't matter what your wife says. I've got the solution to this tricky little dilemma."

Again the living room was filled with silence until the landlady addressed Richard.

"Take off your belt," she ordered.

He removed the belt and held it in both hands.

"Now use it to tie your wife to the chair," she said, grabbing Melanie's hand and pushing her toward the kitchen, the gun pointed at the younger woman's waist.

Mrs. Corvin shoved Melanie into the kitchen chair and waved the gun at Richard's face. "Do it now," she said, "And make it tight."

After he tied Melanie's hands behind the chair, Mrs. Corvin felt the knot. "Good," she said, nodding.

"Now for you," the woman said, aiming the gun at his midsection.

"What are you doing?" Melanie shrieked.

"I'm going to shoot him."

"No!"

"Should I kill you first?"

"They'll know you did it!" Melanie shouted.

"Not after I set the fire."

Melanie grappled with the knotted belt, but wasn't able to free her hands. "Richard!" she yelled.

As the landlady pulled the trigger, Richard lunged forward, directly into the line of fire. Just then, Melanie saw Gertrude dash into the room and blow a strong gust of wind at the gun, knocking it out of Elaine Corvin's hand and causing the bullet to blast a hole in the ceiling, instead of in Richard. The ghost's second burst of cold air slammed her daughter to the floor.

Richard grabbed the gun, which had landed near where he had fallen, and pointed it at the stunned landlady. "What the hell happened just now?" Richard asked Melanie. "Why didn't that bullet hit me?"

"I guess Mrs. Corvin had bad aim," Melanie said, winking at Gertrude.

"But she fell down hard and I didn't even touch her."

"I don't know," Melanie said. "Maybe she tripped. Whatever the reason, we're very lucky to be alive."

Gertrude blew a farewell kiss to Melanie as she faded into the wall and disappeared.

WORDLESS

"What can I get for you?" the deli counter guy asked Ben Stillwater.

"Half pound of ham." That's what Ben meant to say. But those weren't the words that came out of his mouth. "Erka mromb carbla omrix," is what he said out loud.

"Huh?" The deli clerk stared at him.

Ben shook his head and tried again. "Omrix zumph locam nesvil."

"What's wrong with you, pal?" the man behind the counter said, this time sympathetically. "Got something wrong with your head?"

Ben shrugged his shoulders and gave the deli guy a bewildered look. *Why can't I talk right?* Biting his lip, he pointed to the baked ham in the display case.

"Okay," the deli man said. "You want some of this ham. How much? A pound?"

"Vinks erka."

"Less than a pound?"

Ben nodded.

"Half a pound?"

Ben nodded his head up and down.

"A half pound of ham coming up," the clerk said, taking the meat from the display case and then slicing it. "You take care of yourself, buddy," he told Ben as he handed him the zipped plastic bag.

This time, Ben didn't even try to speak. He felt his eyes tearing as he nodded again.

Ben got into his car, closed the door, and practiced talking out loud. But he couldn't say the simplest things—not even his name. Everything sounded like gibberish.

He checked his watch. It was just after eleven o'clock, Saturday morning. *Was Doctor Sanchez in?* Since he couldn't call for an appointment, he drove to the doctor's office in the nearby medical complex.

"Can I help you?" the receptionist asked when Ben approached the counter.

Ben pointed to his throat.

"Oh," the gray-haired woman said. "You can't speak. Laryngitis?"

Ben shrugged his shoulders. *Easier to let her think that.*

"Your name?"

Ben grabbed a pad and pen on the counter and wrote his name. But, as he tore off the sheet, he frowned. The name on the paper wasn't "Ben Stillwater." He had written "Zmovk Lqouvi."

What the hell's wrong with me? Ben crumpled the paper and tried to smile at the receptionist as he reached into his wallet and took out his driver's license. He handed her the card.

"That's you?" she said, examining the license and then looking at him. "You're Benjamin Stillwater?" She glanced at the scrunched piece of paper on the counter.

Ben nodded, pointing to the photo ID next to his name with one hand and scooping up the paper he had written on with the other.

"Yes, I guess that is you." The woman's eyes traveled again to the crumpled wad now in Ben's right hand. "Please stay here while I check with the doctor."

Ben leaned against the counter, waiting for the receptionist to return. He was relieved the room was empty so no one else had witnessed his odd behavior.

He transferred the crushed paper from his hand to his pants pocket, not willing to drop it into the small open trashcan since the receptionist seemed overly curious about what he had written.

"Doctor Sanchez will see you after he finishes with his patient," the woman said as she returned, avoiding eye contact with Ben. "Please have a seat."

Ben sat and picked up a magazine. He glanced at the title—*People*—thankful he could still read. *Will I lose that too?* Nothing seemed certain anymore. He skimmed the pages, stopping at the headline "Celebrity Word Loss Strategies." *Huh?* He read it again. The actual headline was "Celebrity Weight Loss Strategies."

With a sigh, he placed the magazine on the end table and closed his eyes.

"Mr. Stillwater?"

Ben opened his eyes and looked up at the receptionist.

"Dr. Sanchez is ready to see you."

Ben stood and followed the woman through the door to a small examination room in the inner office.

The doctor arrived immediately after. "Hello, Ben," he said, smiling.

Ben was surprised Dr. Sanchez remembered his name—he had seen him only twice. Then he noticed the "Benjamin Stillwater" file in the man's right hand.

"From what Mrs. Rathwell tells me, you're having trouble speaking. Is that correct?"

Ben nodded vigorously.

"Is it laryngitis?"

Ben shook his head.

"Something else then. Let's have a look." Dr. Sanchez motioned to the examination table and Ben hopped onto it.

The doctor checked Ben's throat with a tongue depressor.

"Everything looks fine inside. Try to whisper and explain the problem."

Ben wanted to say, "My words don't come out right." But what he actually said was, "Xhumbi waznu esp gniqv mnavlep cvibz."

"I don't understand." The doctor's bushy eyebrows formed twin arches. "What are you trying to say?"

"Kevzar bliquc." Ben eyes began to tear.

"Do you have some sort of speech problem?"

Ben wiped his eyes with his left hand and nodded.

"If I give you a pencil and paper, can you describe how this happened?"

Ben frowned and shook his head.

"Really?" The doctor stared at Ben. "You can't write either? Show me, please." He grabbed a sheet of paper and a pen from the counter and gave them to Ben. "Write your name."

Ben tried writing his name again and, for the second time, "Ben Stillwater" came out "Zmovk Lqouvi."

"This is truly amazing," Dr. Sanchez said, his thick eyebrows rising as he opened Ben's file and scanned it. "There's nothing here about any speech or writing problems. When did all this start?"

Ben pointed to his watch.

"Today?"

Ben nodded.

"This morning?"

Ben nodded again.

"Is anything else bothering you, like a headache?"

Ben shook his head.

The doctor closed the file. "I want you to take a CT scan, and then an MRI, right now," he said. "You're young and don't have any symptoms. But, just in case, I have to rule out a stroke."

A dark-haired nurse took Ben first to the CT scan room and then the MRI chamber, both times positioning him in the front of waiting patients, which earned angry glares. Afterwards, he returned to Dr. Sanchez's office while the doctor reviewed the results.

"The tests were negative," Dr. Sanchez told Ben. "As I thought, it's not a stroke or any other physical condition that I can find."

Ben opened his hands, palms up and gave the doctor a questioning look.

"I'm sorry, son, but I don't know what's wrong with you."

Dr. Sanchez took out his prescription pad and started writing. "I'm sending you to an associate of mine—a neurologist who specializes in language disorders. I want Doctor Malcomb to examine you and run some more tests. I'll have Mrs. Rathwell make an emergency appointment so Doctor Malcomb will see you today and I'll give you a letter so you won't have to explain anything."

Dr. Sanchez grabbed Ben's shoulders and smiled at him. "Don't worry, Ben. We'll find out what's happened to you and then we'll fix it."

At two o'clock, Ben sat in Dr. Malcomb's office, waiting for her to finish reading Dr. Sanchez's letter. The envelope had been sealed and he hadn't had any desire to open it. There was no reason to; he knew the problem. *Could she fix it?*

Dr. Malcomb was a stunning brunette—someone yesterday's Ben would have wanted to date. But, in his current condition, he couldn't fully appreciate the doctor's looks.

Dr. Malcomb lowered the paper and gazed at Ben with cobalt blue eyes. "This is very unusual," she said. "I know you can't talk or write, but I need some information so please shake or nod your head to answer. Okay?"

Ben nodded.

"Did you have any recent head injury?"

Ben shook his head.

"No car accident or fall?"

Ben shook his head again.

"Any illness—maybe the flu or a virus?"

Ben shook his head.

"Are you taking any new medications?"

As he shook his head, Ben felt like a bobblehead doll.

Dr. Malcomb stood, resting her hands on the desk.

Ben tried not to stare, but even the shapeless lab coat couldn't hide the doctor's perfect figure.

"Okay," she said. "Let's run all the tests and see if we can find out what's causing your problems."

Ben left Dr. Malcomb's office with no new information about his baffling condition. The doctor had promised to rush the lab work so she'd have the results Tuesday morning—but that was still three days.

What to do till then? Ben wondered as he stepped into the car. He could easily avoid being around people for the rest of the weekend, but Monday morning was work. *Can't call in sick. Can't explain what's wrong. Can't even write a note...Shit!*

He banged his fist on the steering wheel. *Like a baby, a 29-year-old baby.* Then he dashed out of the car and back to Dr. Malcomb's office.

"Did you forget something, Mr. Stillwater?" the receptionist asked.

Ben made a writing motion with his fingers.

"You want to write something?" the young woman asked. "Do you need paper?"

Ben shook his head. Then he grabbed one of Dr. Malcomb's

business cards from the counter display and shoved it in front of the receptionist's eyeglasses.

"You need to see the doctor again?"

Ben smiled and nodded.

"She's with another patient now. I'm sorry, but you'll have to wait until she's done."

Ben sat and waited.

"What's wrong?" Dr. Malcomb asked when Ben entered her office.

Again he pretended to write. *Like playing charades all the time.*

"You need me to write something?"

He nodded and clapped his hands.

"What should I write?"

How to explain? Ben motioned like he was getting dressed—putting on pants, shirt, and tie. Then, noticing the doctor's attaché case on the floor against the desk, he picked it up and walked a few steps.

"Job!" Dr. Malcomb shouted, much like a charades player who had just figured out a tough word. "You need a letter for work!"

Ben nodded his head vigorously.

"What kind of work do you do?"

Ben moved to the doctor's desk and pretended to unfurl a large piece of paper. Then, after studying the room, he made believe he was using a tape measure on the walls and floor.

"You're a painter?"

Ben shook his head.

"A builder?"

Ben shook his head, but waved his hands.

"Like a builder?"

Ben nodded and again pretended to unravel a paper on the desk.

"An architect?"

Ben nodded, again waving his hands.

"Not quite an architect? You work for an architect?"

Ben nodded, glad Dr. Malcomb was good at charades.

"I'm guessing you don't have a business card or anything with the name of the company."

Ben shook his head.

"That's okay. I'll write a 'To Whom It May Concern' note and give you a copy of Dr. Sanchez's letter too. That should be enough to explain the problem. Okay?"

Ben nodded.

Ben's condition didn't improve when he got home late Saturday afternoon. Whenever he tried to talk, gibberish came out of his mouth. He couldn't write either; the letters he scribbled still didn't form words.

He turned off his phone and found the Mets/Nationals game on TV. But even though he was a Mets fan, he stopped watching the 1-1 game in the eighth inning, unable to enjoy it, and went to bed.

When Ben woke up Sunday morning, he immediately tried speaking aloud. "Gleizah," he said instead of "hello" and threw the pillow on the floor in frustration.

After turning on his phone, Ben listened to his messages. He had three—two from his mother and one from his friend, Greg. His mother's second message was disturbing.

"Why didn't you return my call?" she whined. "You told me you didn't have anything planned tonight and you were just going to stay home and take it easy. So now it's nine o'clock and you're not answering. If I don't hear from you, I'm coming over tomorrow morning."

Shit! Ben jumped out of bed, got dressed, and ate a quick breakfast of Cheerios. Then he made copies of his two doctor notes. When he was finished, he turned on the TV, sat on the couch, and waited for Mom.

Ben didn't have to wait very long. At nine-thirty, his doorbell rang. He rushed to the door and, without even bothering to check the peephole, flung it open. His mother, a former actress, stood there—dressed as if she were heading directly to the stage.

"Oh, thank God you're okay!" she cried, wrapping her thin arms around Ben's neck. "Why didn't you call me like I asked?"

Ben pointed to his throat and shook his head.

"You can't talk? Something's wrong with your throat?"

Dragging his mother inside, Ben pointed to the two letters on the coffee table.

"Those are for me?" she asked.

Ben nodded.

His mother picked up the papers and read them. When she finished, she studied Ben's face carefully. "Is all this really true? You can't talk or write?"

"Ugdohlp."

His mother held her hand to her mouth and groaned theatrically. "How could something like this happen?"

"Vxrhinq bvez." Ben shrugged.

She pointed to one of the papers. "Does this speech doctor know how fix it?"

Ben shrugged again.

"I've never heard of anybody having a problem like this. There must be something wrong with your head. I'm going to call Horace. His wife's cousin is a brain surgeon."

"Hbknaad!"

Although Ben's word didn't make sense, his mother understood the anger in his voice. He scowled at her and shook his head.

"Okay, I won't call Horace. But I have to do something. You can't just stay in your apartment and hide. Oh God!" She pointed at Ben. "The other letter...Of course, you can't go to work like this. You have to take time off and they'll have to pay you disability."

Ben's mother sat on the couch and put her hands over her head. "This is horrible, really dreadful." She looked up and stared at him. "I should stay here with you until you can talk again—answer your phone, be your interpreter, help out. Your father will understand."

Ben shook his head.

"But how will you manage?"

Ben waved his hands gently, which he hoped indicated that he could take care of himself. He didn't want his mother moving in with him. *Like a baby!*

It took several more hand motions, nods, and smiles to reassure her he would be all right. In the doorway, she kissed Ben and repeated her willingness to move in with him. "I'll stop in every morning until you're better," she promised as she left. Ben closed the door and leaned against it.

He had convinced his mother that he'd be all right. Now all he had to do was convince himself.

Ben was half-watching a dopey Comedy Central movie Sunday afternoon when he heard a knock on the door. Gazing through the peephole, he saw a young dark-haired woman.

I've seen her before, Ben realized as he opened the door. *But where?*

"Hi," the brunette said, smiling. "Remember me? I'm Robin from Dr. Sanchez's office. I took you to the CT scan and MRI yesterday."

Ben nodded. Then he spread out his hands, palms up, and gave her his best questioning look.

"The doctor left a message on your phone about an hour ago. Did you get it?"

Ben shook his head.

"Dr. Sanchez figured you turned off your phone because you can't talk so that's why he sent me here. You have to go to the office—right now."

Ben shrugged and again gave her a puzzled look.

"I'm sorry, but I can't explain. You just have to come."

Ben took Robin by the arm and pulled her into his kitchen, stopping in front of a calendar on the wall. He pointed to a word on the top left: "SUNDAY."

"I know," she said. "Today is Sunday. But something has happened and that's why the doctor is in his office."

Ben grabbed his jacket and followed Robin outside.

There were at least ten cars parked near the entrance of the medical complex that led to Dr. Sanchez's office. Ben pulled into a space and hurried up the steps, just a few feet behind Robin.

"Here he is," she announced, flinging open the office door.

Ben entered the waiting room and saw the doctor leaning against the wall and seven people—different sizes, shapes, and colors—seated in the chairs. He noticed an overweight young black man, a middle-aged blonde woman, a skinny teenage boy with acne, an Asian woman with a heavily lined face, and...

"Yvblort," the black guy said.

Ben stared at the big fellow in amazement. The man had spoken gibberish—and Ben had understood him.

"Ucymsta," Ben said, returning the greeting.

The young man smiled at him.

"Vqictz noplim wrembo eku?" the blonde lady asked.

"Razcub," Ben said, nodding that, yes, he had understood her.

"So you can all communicate with Ben?" Dr. Sanchez asked.

The others nodded at him.

"And none of you can write words?"

They all nodded again.

The doctor shook his head. "I don't know what's going on, but, whatever it is, it seems to be happening everywhere. All over the world, people are waking up with the same condition you have. They can't speak or write their language anymore. It's like an epidemic."

"Zwigo dax cuipb ebip?" the little Asian lady asked.

Ben knew her question was, "Will it go away?" However, the doctor didn't quite get it.

"I don't know how many other people are affected," he said. "We'll just have to wait and see."

"Noce vrigbaq emoz domta svumj," the pimply-faced teen said, smiling.

Ben looked at the boy and nodded. Maybe it was kind of cool, this strange new language that he and these seven people—and apparently many others—shared.

Dr. Sanchez turned on the waiting room TV, picked up the remote, and surfed the channels. Nearly every station was airing a special news report. He stayed on CNN where a frightened-looking man with sunglasses stood outside a church, identified on screen as being in Atlanta.

"...throughout the city and spreading fast," he said, into his microphone. "In churches and restaurants—there're people everywhere that're talking this weird way and writing stuff that we can't understand. But they can read it—and others like them know what the writing means." He shook his head. "Laura, I've never seen anything like this. It's truly bizarre."

The picture shifted to a perplexed-looking blonde anchor-woman. "Thanks, Jordan. No one understands what's going on yet. We've contacted doctors and they're swamped with frightened patients, but they don't have any answers." She faced the camera. "Stay tuned to CNN for further updates on this new language crisis."

Dr. Sanchez turned off the TV and shook his head. "I really don't have any answers either," he began. "We'll have to bvrwc gvac minhr..."

The doctor grasped his throat, horrified at the strange sounds he was making.

"Oh, no," Robin moaned, covering her mouth with her hands.

"Eqic vuin zaku soh gyul," the little Asian woman said, reaching out to pat the doctor's hand.

Ben nodded his head in agreement. He wasn't scared any more. It was a drastic change, but, when the conversion was completed, everything would be all right. *A brand new international language...*

DARE TO DREAM

"You are the most beautiful woman in the world," Count Fabrio whispered into Mary McGavin's ear as they sat closely together on the deck of his yacht, watching a glorious violet sunset fade into the Aegean Sea. "Marry me so we can always be together."

"Yes," Mary said. "Of course I will marry you."

Mary opened her eyes, stretched her arms, and smiled. Count Fabrio was a particular favorite of her dream characters. He was handsome, respectful, kind—all the qualities she wanted in a man. Maybe she couldn't have someone like that in her everyday life, but the count was the man of her dreams—literally.

She rolled over in bed to check the clock and saw that the alarm was about to sound. It was time to get ready for work.

Mary wasn't crazy about her job. Being a bank teller was boring, especially after thirty-seven years. But she knew she was fortunate to still have a job. With so many people now banking online, Central Savings had fired all the full-time tellers except for the two with the most seniority: herself and Sally Ann Pomeroy.

Oh well. Mary reluctantly stepped out of bed. *I get to dream again tonight.*

After another long and uneventful workday, Mary returned to her small apartment. She microwaved a Swedish meatballs dinner and ate while watching Channel 7 Eyewitness News. As usual, the reports were depressing—a local highway car crash had killed two, a hurricane was battering Florida, and a suicide bomber had blown up five innocent shoppers in a London department store.

Mary turned off the TV and picked up *Cops on the Run,* a thriller about two police officers—a man and a woman—being chased by gangsters. The novel was exciting so Mary read until ten o'clock. Then, yawning, she put the book aside and prepared for bed.

Under the covers, Mary closed her eyes and readied herself for her nightly dream. *I hope it's Fabrio again...*

The sounds of swirling winds and heavy rain pelting the windows disturbed Mary. *A storm?* she wondered as she opened her eyes. The skies had been clear when she went to bed and she didn't remember any rain in the weather forecast.

Mary stepped to the window and peered outside. Except for the cascades of pouring rain, it was too dark to see much else. But what she did see was shocking.

A large palm tree swayed dangerously near her window, its long segmented trunk looking like it could snap at any time.

Mary gasped. *Palm tree?* She lived in Queens in New York City—a place with no tropical trees. Slowly, she backed into the bed and sat. *How could this happen?*

As the wind continued to roar, Mary heard sirens in the distance, followed by the blare of a megaphone. "All residents must evacuate! You cannot remain in your home during the hurricane!"

Hurricane? That was in Florida.

There was a tremendous crash on the roof and the impact knocked Mary onto the floor. Books flew off the shelf near her bed, one hardcover volume missing Mary's head by inches.

She crawled into bed, placed the pillow over her head, and closed her eyes. *Must be a dream. But it's so real.*

When Mary opened her eyes, she immediately rushed to the window. It was early morning with no rain or heavy winds. She recognized the apartment building and the Key Food supermarket across the street. The swaying palm tree was gone.

No more TV news at night, Mary vowed.

As she headed to the bathroom, she noticed several hardcover books lying askew on the bedroom floor. Shaking her head, she picked up the volumes and placed them in the bookcase.

That evening, Mary watched a DVD of *Pretty Woman* and then read three chapters of *Cops on the Run*. The novel was getting even more exciting. Vanessa and Devin had once again outwitted the Nardi gang and were hiding in the barn of an abandoned farm.

She closed the book and immediately fell asleep.

Mary grimaced as she opened her eyes. Somehow, her bed was extremely uncomfortable. She touched what should have been the mattress and discovered she was no longer in a bed. Instead, she was lying on top of a pile of musty-smelling hay. And she was no longer at home; she was in an old gray barn.

"Glad you finally woke up," a young blond man in a police uniform said to her.

She stared at the policeman's nametag and pointed. "You're..."

"The name's Devin O'Neill."

"That's impossible," Mary said, sitting up. "You're not real. You're just a character in a book I'm reading."

"Oh yeah?" Devin said. "I feel pretty real to me. But there's no time to talk. We've got to move fast before Nardi and the others find the three of us."

"Three?"

"My partner's waiting for us outside."

"This can't be happening," Mary whispered as she followed Devin. She immediately recognized Vanessa Franklin, Devin's petite African-American partner, who faced the abandoned fields.

"Shh," Vanessa said when Devin and Mary reached her. "The Nardi gang's coming. Listen."

Mary could hear engine sounds in the distance. "What are you going to do now?" she asked. She hadn't read this scene.

"Our car is dead so we can't run," Devin said. "We've got to stay here and fight."

"But there're six of them," Mary pointed out.

Devin shrugged. "We've got no other choice." He reached into his jacket, took out a gun, and handed it to Mary. "Here," he said. "You can help us."

"But I don't know how to shoot a gun," Mary said.

"Just aim like this and then pull the trigger," Vanessa said, demonstrating with her weapon. "There's no time to teach you now. We've got to find cover."

Mary, Devin, and Vanessa hid behind the side of the barn, shoving two bales of rotted hay in front of them for additional protection.

"This smells awful," Mary complained.

"Quiet," Vanessa ordered. "Our only chance is to surprise Nardi so stick your head down and shut up."

Mary did as she was told. Less than five minutes later, she heard a car approach and stop nearby.

"Get ready," Vanessa whispered.

The doors of the car opened and, as Mary peeked over the rancid hay, she counted six swarthy men. Each wore a black suit and carried a gun or rifle.

"Now!" Vanessa shouted. Jumping up, she fired her gun at the gangsters.

As shots reverberated in all directions, Mary ducked again,

covering her head with her hands and crying.

"I'm hit!" Devin shouted. He slithered down, leaned against Mary's shoulder, and she felt warm blood oozing onto her shirt.

Mary closed her eyes tightly and prayed hard. *Wake up...I want to stop dreaming and wake up!*

When Mary opened her eyes, she saw the white ceiling of her bedroom. *Home!* She felt like kissing the familiar walls. Devin, Vanessa, the barn, the gangsters, the guns—they were all gone. *Just another scary dream.*

Mary reached down and touched her nightgown. It felt sticky. Pulling off the blanket, she saw the bottom sheet was covered with blood. "No!" she shouted, jumping out of bed.

Mary called the bank, leaving a message that she was sick—not a lie because she certainly wasn't in shape to go to work.

She spent the morning wandering through stores in the nearby shopping center, just buying a few entertainment magazines. After lunch at Burger King, she went to Key Food and bought lettuce, an orange, and a box of Triscuits before returning to her apartment.

Mary watched *Seinfeld* reruns till dinner and then DVDs of two of her favorite old movies—*Tootsie* and *When Harry Met Sally*.

She started to get ready for bed, but, as she brushed her teeth, Mary changed her mind. Instead, she made a cup of instant coffee, picked up *People* magazine, wrapped herself in a blanket on the couch, and read.

With the help of four cups of coffee, Mary managed to stay awake for the entire night. In the morning, she showered, dressed, and headed off to work.

"What's wrong with you?" Sally Ann Pomeroy asked as the customer left Mary's window. "You were out yesterday. Are you still sick?"

Mary and Sally Ann had been coworkers at Central Savings

for many years, but they were not friends. Mary thought Sally Ann resembled a weasel—both in appearance and behavior.

"I'm just not sleeping well," Mary admitted. She had felt okay in the morning. But by afternoon, lack of sleep had hit her like a sledgehammer and she had made several silly mistakes.

"Maybe you should go home early," Sally Ann suggested.

"I'll be okay."

Sally Ann didn't look convinced. "Are you sure? You almost gave Mr. Fitzsimmons an extra hundred dollars."

"But I caught it in time."

"You never do things like that."

"I'll be all right, Sally Ann. Drop it."

"If you say so." Sally Ann shrugged and turned her pointy face away.

Mary managed to get through the rest of the afternoon without making any more mistakes. When she went home, she knew she had to get some sleep. But she was very afraid.

Mary opened her eyes and gazed up at the star-filled sky. She recognized the gleaming wood railings of Count Fabrio's luxurious yacht and felt the waves swaying gently beneath her. Mary smiled. *A good dream.*

"You are awake, my dear?" Count Fabrio asked from the adjoining lounge chair.

"Yes," Mary said.

"I am glad." The count nodded. "We have much to do tonight."

"Oh?" His words surprised her. In the other Fabrio dreams, all they had done was cruise in the yacht while the count kissed her tenderly and told her how much he loved her. It had been simple, but wonderful.

"You don't remember?" he asked.

"No."

"Then I will remind you. The shipment is below and we must

deliver it before morning. You are to pose as my wife and you will distract the port authorities while I do the rest."

"What are we delivering?" Mary asked.

"Weapons."

"Guns?"

"Of course." Count Fabrio scowled at her. "How could you forget? We talked about the arrangement the last time you were on board. You argued about your fee before I agreed to pay you a million U.S. dollars."

"But I don't want your money!" Mary cried. "I don't want to do this!"

"What is the matter with you, Mary? The rebel army is depending on this shipment. We will land within the hour."

Mary closed her eyes tightly, blinked furiously, and then opened them, hoping to wake from the dream. However, when she focused again, Fabrio was still glaring at her. The count's handsome chiseled features had turned stony.

"We must prepare now," he said, reaching for Mary's arm.

"No!" She shoved his hand away and tried to run.

But the much stronger Fabrio held onto Mary's shoulder. Then he twisted her arms behind her back and shoved her against the railing.

"I won't do it!" she yelled.

"Then I must dispose of you."

"Please," Mary begged. "You told me how much you loved me and that you wanted to marry me."

"That was another woman, another Mary. You are not the same person and, if you will not cooperate, then you are worthless to me." With one quick motion, he lifted Mary above the polished railing and heaved her into the swirling sea.

"No!" Mary shouted. "Fabrio, please! I can't swim!"

"Goodbye," he said, stepping away from the railing.

Officer Hector Ramos lifted his head from Mary's face as his partner sat on the closed toilet seat cradling her limp nightgown-clad body. "I think she's gone," Officer Ramos whispered.

The policemen had been summoned to Mary McGavin's apartment at midnight when water from her flooded bathroom had leaked through the downstairs neighbor's ceiling. After they turned off the faucets and pulled Mary from the overflowing bathtub, Officer Ramos had tried mouth-to-mouth resuscitation.

"You did your best," his older partner said.

"But it doesn't make any sense," Officer Ramos continued.

"It never makes sense for someone to die like this, drowning in a bathtub, and she's dressed so it probably wasn't an accident. She must've wanted to kill herself."

"That's not what I meant," Officer Ramos said.

"Huh?"

"This is a bathtub in an apartment—and all the water is regular tap water, right?"

"Of course it is."

Officer Ramos shook his head. "But the water in this lady's mouth, the water that I tasted—it's not tap water. It's salt water."

JEREMY'S TOYS

Jeremy knelt on the floor of his room, giving rides to his superheroes. "Zoom!" he shouted as he raced Spiderman in a Hot Wheels car along the Lego road he had built between his bed and bookshelf. Then he found Batman and the Batmobile and gave the Caped Crusader a ride too.

When he wasn't in school, Jeremy spent lots of time in his room by himself. At first, he had been sad and mad. But then Grannie had explained why she and Grampie couldn't play with him.

"We love you very much," Grannie had said. "But Grampie and I have to work and make money to take care of you so we don't have time to play." Then she had kissed him on the forehead and left the house to go to her job, cleaning other people's houses.

Grampie was home now, but he had been working at the store so he was very tired. Jeremy knew he could wake up Grampie if he ever needed help, but he tried to be a good boy and let his grandfather sleep.

Jeremy checked the digital clock on his bookshelf. Even though he was only six-years-old, he knew how to tell time. It was 5:38 now so he could go into the kitchen and eat the dinner Grannie had made for him. All he had to do was open the refrigerator and take out the cup of milk and chicken sandwich. Then he could use the stepstool to open the freezer and have a strawberry ice cream bar for dessert.

After dinner, Jeremy was allowed to turn on the TV and watch cartoons till 7:30. Then, if Grampie was still sleeping, he had to wake his grandfather so he could give Jeremy a bath. Afterwards, Grampie would read him a bedtime story, tuck him into bed, and kiss him goodnight.

Sometime during the night, while Jeremy slept, Grannie would come home and Grampie would go to work. In the morning, Grannie would wake Jeremy, make him a yummy hot breakfast, and get him ready for school.

Jeremy knew the other boys and girls had mommies and daddies. He also knew many of the kids got together to play after school. He didn't have a mommy or daddy and he didn't play with kids after school. But he had Grannie and Grampie—and he had his toys.

One late afternoon, Jeremy sat on the floor of his room reading his favorite book, *Caps for Sale*, for the hundredth time. He didn't know how to read yet, but he did know most of the words of the book by heart, so, as he turned the pages, he pretended to read the story out loud.

When he finished, he closed the book and looked at his toy cabinet, deciding what he wanted to do next.

"Why don't you give me a ride on the tractor?" a man's voice said.

Jeremy turned his head, trying to figure out where the words were coming from. It didn't sound like any of his talking toys.

"I'm over here," the voice said. "With the trucks."

Jeremy walked to the plastic bin that housed his cars and trucks and peered inside. He noticed a farmer doll sitting in a green tractor.

"Yup, you found me."

Jeremy stared at the little farmer in the tractor. The voice was coming from that figure. But the farmer wasn't a talking toy.

"You can talk?" Jeremy asked.

"Yup," the farmer said. "I sure can."

"Then how come you never said anything before?"

"Maybe I didn't have anything to say," the farmer said, chuckling. "Hey, let's go for a ride around my farm."

That sounded like a good idea to Jeremy. "Okay," he said. "I'll make a farm." After he found a big red barn and some yellow fencing, he placed a horse, cow, and pig in the enclosure and pushed the farmer in the tractor around the floor.

"That was lots of fun," the farmer said when Jeremy finished playing with the farm.

"Yeah," Jeremy agreed. "Is it okay if I put you away now and do something else?"

"Sure," the farmer said. "I'll talk to you again soon."

When Jeremy returned to his room the next day after school, he thought about playing with the talking farmer. He picked up the little man, still sitting in the tractor.

"Hello," Jeremy said to the farmer.

But the smiling toy man didn't respond.

Jeremy tossed the farmer and tractor into the bin and reached for his crayons.

"Hey!" a girl's voice called. "Let's play my game."

Jeremy frowned. He didn't remember having a girl doll. *That was for babies.*

"I'm not a doll, silly," the voice said, even though Jeremy hadn't spoken. "I already told you I'm a game."

Jeremy moved to the shelf that held his games. The top one was Candy Land. He opened the box and unfolded the board.

"You're close," the girl's voice said. "I'm right in here."

Jeremy looked at the four little plastic pieces inside the box. One of the characters was a gingerbread girl.

"Is this you?" he asked, tapping the orange figure.

"Yes," she said. "Now please stop tickling me and choose one of my friends so we can play."

Jeremy took the teal ice cream cone and placed both characters on the colorful game board. Even though Jeremy had to spin the arrow for all the turns and then move both pieces, he liked playing with the talking gingerbread girl.

They played two games; Jeremy won the first and the gingerbread girl won the second.

"That was fun," Jeremy said as he folded the board and tucked the spinner and all the pieces inside the Candy Land box.

"Yes," the gingerbread girl agreed. "Thanks for playing my game."

❧❧

When Jeremy woke up Saturday morning, he was excited, wondering which of his toys would talk to him. He sat in his bed and waited.

But none of the toys spoke.

After a few minutes, Jeremy grew impatient. "Hey!" he called, scanning the room. "Don't any of you guys want to play with me today?"

"Just wait a minute," a gruff man's voice said. "I've got to finish cleaning my engine."

"Huh?"

"You heard me, kid. I'm cleaning myself."

"Who are you?"

"I'll give you a hint. Listen to this."

Jeremy heard a loud "Chug! Chug!" sound. "I know!" he said, excitedly. "You're a train!"

"Not just a train. I'm the locomotive, the one that pulls all the cars of the train. C'mon! I'm ready now. Let's go take a ride."

Jeremy played with the talking locomotive and his other toys till it was time for dinner.

At school Monday morning, Jeremy's teacher stood in front of the room holding hands with a dark-skinned little girl with pigtails whom Jeremy had never seen before.

"This is Angela," Mrs. Jackson said. "She will be joining our class. Everyone say 'hello' to Angela."

When Jeremy mouthed his greeting, he saw Angela smile at him and he returned her smile.

Mrs. Jackson placed Angela in the seat next to Jeremy, which had been empty since mean Tommy Narbone moved away. Tommy had poked Jeremy with his pencil and kicked him if he put his feet anywhere near Tommy's desk.

"Jeremy," Mrs. Jackson said. "I want you to be Angela's buddy and help her if she needs anything. Okay?"

Jeremy nodded.

For the rest of the morning, Angela didn't ask Jeremy for any help, but every time he snuck a peek at the girl, she smiled.

When it was time for lunch, Jeremy grabbed his lunchbox and stood, preparing to get on line.

"Can I eat lunch with you?" Angela asked him, smiling again.

"Sure," Jeremy replied. He usually ate lunch alone.

As they sat next to each other on the cafeteria bench, Angela talked steadily, peppering Jeremy with questions. "I like to ride my bike. Do you have a bike? Do you like to ride it?"

"Yes, I have a bike," Jeremy said. He didn't tell her that he didn't ride much because he didn't want to wake Grampie just to watch him.

Angela changed the subject. "I like to draw, mostly animals. I have a cat named Patches so I color lots of cat pictures. What things do you like to draw?"

"Cars and trains."

"I like to draw cars and trains too, and also trucks and buses."

"You do?" Jeremy was surprised. "But you're a girl."

Angela laughed hard, spitting out some of her milk. "You're funny," she said as she wiped her mouth with a napkin. "Lots of girls like cars and trucks. I've got plenty of them in my new house. Maybe you could come over and play."

"Yeah," Jeremy said, smiling. "That would be fun."

Angela reached into the pocket of her jeans. "My mom wrote her phone number so I could give it to a new friend." She handed Jeremy a small strip of paper. "Here," she said. "Your mom can call my mom."

"I don't have a mom," Jeremy said, looking at the phone number.

"Who lives in your house with you?"

"My grandmother and grandfather."

"That's okay," Angela said. "Tell them to call my mom."

When Jeremy got off the school bus, he hugged Grannie and then gave her Angela's paper. "Can you call Angela's mom so I can go over her house?" he asked.

"A new friend?" Grannie said, ruffling Jeremy's curly brown hair. "I'll call right now."

Jeremy ate a banana while Grannie stood in the kitchen talking to Angela's mom. He heard his grandmother explain who she was and then watched her listen, smile, and nod.

"That sounds great, Joanne," Grannie said. "Thanks so much for inviting Jeremy. He'll take the bus home with Angela tomorrow afternoon and my husband, Scott, will pick him up."

That afternoon, Jeremy played with talking Batman and his Batmobile, racing around the room helping the Caped Crusader save people in trouble.

"Bye," he said to the superhero as he returned him to the shelf. "I won't be back home till later tomorrow."

"Oh," Batman said in his deep baritone. "What're you doing tomorrow?"

"I'm playing with my friend, Angela."

"Great!" Batman shouted. "Have a good time."

"Thanks, I will."

Jeremy liked Angela's house. It had high ceilings, big rooms, and lots of windows. Best of all, Angela's mom baked chocolate chip cookies, which they ate while Patches the cat patrolled the floor, occasionally rubbing against Jeremy's legs and purring.

After snack, Jeremy and Angela played with her toys. He especially liked the garbage truck that had a pail you could fill with pretend garbage and toss into the opening in the back, like the real truck on his street.

They also played Candy Land and, this time, Jeremy didn't have to do all the spinning and move both plastic pieces around the board. They each took turns.

When Grampie came to take him home for dinner, Jeremy had an idea. "Can Angela take the bus to my house?" he asked both Angela's mother and Grampie.

"Is that okay with you?" Angela's mom asked Grampie.

"Sure," he said.

They made a date for Thursday afternoon. Jeremy knew that was in two days. He was excited about showing Angela his talking toys.

On Wednesday night, before going to sleep, Jeremy made sure his room was neat and clean, with all his toys in place. Grannie and Grampie had already straightened out the rest of the house. They knew Jeremy wanted everything to look nice for Angela.

On Thursday afternoon, Angela got on Jeremy's bus with him and they rode together to Jeremy's house. "Oh, this is neat!" she squealed when they got off the bus. "Your house is so cute!"

That's what Jeremy liked most about Angela. She thought everything was great, even his little house.

For snack, Grannie gave them orange juice and lemon cookies—they weren't homemade, but they tasted good anyway. Then they went to Jeremy's room to play.

"I've got some special toys to show you," he told Angela.

"Really? What's special about them?"

"You'll see. Just stand here and wait."

They stood inside the doorway and waited. But nothing happened.

"It's taking a long time, Angela said. "Maybe we can just play something while we wait...I like that police car." She took the car out of Jeremy's bin and started rolling it on the floor. "Let's have a race."

"Okay," Jeremy said. He grabbed a red Hot Wheels and knelt on the floor next to Angela. They played three times with Angela winning all the races because Jeremy couldn't concentrate. He kept looking around the room, waiting for one of his toys to say something.

"What's the matter?" Angela asked after the third race.

"I wanted to show you what my toys can do," Jeremy said.

"I see what they can do."

"I mean the special thing."

Angela gave him a puzzled look.

"My toys talk to me," Jeremy explained.

"I don't hear any toy talking."

"Well, they do."

Angela laughed and poked Jeremy in the arm. "You're so silly," she said. "Let's play Chutes & Ladders. I bet I can beat you."

Jeremy and Angela spent the rest of the afternoon playing together. During that time, none of Jeremy's toys talked to them. In fact, the toys never said anything else to Jeremy, even when he was alone.

As time passed, Jeremy hardly remembered that his toys had once spoken to him. He was too busy playing with Angela and the other friends he made in school.

THE SEA CRYSTAL

"Ooh!" Kayla Godfrey gushed as she picked up the odd-looking crystal formation wedged inside the black rocks. "Dan, take a look at this one."

Her husband slogged through the mushy sand and climbed next to Kayla. "What is it?" he asked.

"I don't know." As she twirled the smoky rectangular crystal in her hands, it caught the sun's rays and seemed to change colors, radiating a soft orange. "It must be some kind of quartz. But it's got bumps and funny lines—very different, don't you think?" She handed the crystal to Dan.

"Maybe it's been affected by the sea," he said, pointing to the turquoise waves of the Caribbean that lashed against the jutting rocks. "Let's bring it back to the ship with the rest of the shells and stones. We should leave now so we can shower and get ready for dinner." He nodded toward the open ferry sitting at the island's dock, half-filled with people. "If we hurry, we can probably make this tender."

Kayla stood in front of the little cabin sink, washing the shells and stones she and Dan had collected on the island. When she rinsed the crystal, she stopped and lifted the piece to examine it.

"Dan," she called. "That bumpy crystal thing changed color again when I washed it. Now it's a light blue."

Her husband stared at the translucent formation in Kayla's hands. "Very weird," he said. "Maybe it's valuable. We can bring it to the ship's jewelry store before dinner and they might be able to tell us what it is."

"Do you think it's worth a lot of money?"

Dan shrugged. "I haven't a clue. But this thing is so different that there's a chance it could be some kind of rare stone people would pay for."

Kayla placed the crystal under the water again. "If that's true, then it should be as clean as possible. I'm going to rinse it some more."

The jeweler in Ocean Gems removed the loupe from his eye and gently lowered the crystal onto the display counter. "I've never seen anything like this before," he told Kayla and Dan. "Where did you say you found it?"

"In the rocks in the water today at the island," Kayla said.

The man shrugged and fingered his goatee. "Well, it certainly is different."

"We thought you might want to buy it for the store," Dan said. "It changes color all the time too. It was orange, then blue, and now it's a pale purple."

"Mauve," Kayla corrected.

"Whatever. Someone must want a crystal like this," Dan continued.

The jeweler shook his head. "Although it's really quite an unusual piece, I have no way of knowing if I could sell it." He lifted the crystal and turned it around in his hands. "And it's not very attractive with all these irregular bumps and markings so, even if I did manage to sell your stone, it wouldn't be for much."

"But all the different colors," Dan persisted. "Look. Now it's some kind of yellow green."

"Lime," Kayla said.

"Thank you, my color expert."

"Changing colors isn't enough of a selling card," the man said, carefully placing the crystal in Dan's hands. "People like pretty objects. I appreciate you letting me look at your find, but I'm afraid it's not something for our store. I suggest you just keep it as an interesting souvenir."

When they arrived at the ship's main restaurant, Kayla and Dan discovered there was a thirty-minute wait for a table for two. "After visiting the island, everyone wants to eat dinner at the same time," the young Asian hostess explained. "But if you don't mind sharing a table, I can seat you right away."

"What do you want to do?" Dan asked.

"I'm starving," Kayla replied. "So let's go share."

They were ushered to a rectangular table for four near the center of the huge room. An African-American man and woman in their early forties occupied two of the seats.

"Good evening," the man said, rising to shake Dan's hand. "I'm Omar Singleton." He nodded to the attractive woman next to him. "And this is my wife, Lisette."

"Glad to meet you," Dan said. "My name's Dan Godfrey."

"Hi. I'm Kayla." She smiled at the other couple.

The four tablemates started talking. Dan and Kayla discovered they had much in common with Omar and Lisette. All four were about the same age and both couples had two children attending college. They all lived in the suburbs—the Godfreys outside Chicago and the Singletons in northern New Jersey.

They continued talking throughout dinner. As they finished dessert, Kayla reached into her pocketbook for a lipstick and noticed the bag containing the crystal. "Oh," she said. "I want to show you this. We found it today in the rocks by the water while exploring the island." She unwrapped the crystal and set it on the table.

"What a strange stone," Lisette said. "It's such a bright red. Is it hot?"

"No," Kayla said, petting the crystal. "But it changes colors all the time."

"Can I hold it?" Lisette asked.

"Sure." Kayla handed her the crystal across the table. As Lisette took it, a flash of light illuminated both women's arms.

"What just happened?" Omar asked, turning to his wife. "Are you okay?"

"I'm fine," Lisette said as she examined the red crystal. "But I have no idea what that was."

"Me neither," Kayla said, staring at her fingers. "Did you see that, Dan?"

"Yeah," her husband said. "For just a moment, your arm turned red."

Before they left the dinner table, the Godfreys and Singletons exchanged room numbers, promising to call each other in the morning. The ship was docking at St. Thomas and they planned to shop together after breakfast.

"Want to eat with us?" Dan asked Omar.

"I'm not sure about that." He gently poked Lisette's arm. "This one moves like a snail when she first gets up."

"That's fine," Kayla said, laughing. "The ship's in port all day so just call us when you're ready to go."

Since Kayla and Dan had an inside cabin, when she woke up in the dark room, Kayla had no idea of the time. She checked the alarm clock next to her bed and the numbers read 7:46.

Better get up, she told herself as she plodded to the bathroom and flipped the light switch. When Kayla saw her face in the mirror, she screamed.

"What's wrong?" Dan asked, sitting up in bed.

"Look at me!" Kayla shouted. Turning on the room light, she stepped in front of Dan.

He stared at his wife in horror. Her skin had changed color. She was no longer a white woman; now she was black.

For a minute, neither of them said anything. Then Kayla started crying. "It has to be the crystal," she said, tears rolling down her black cheeks. "Last night, when I gave it to Lisette—that red light."

Dan pointed at her. "And you're the same shade of black as Lisette."

"Do you think the same thing happened to her?"

Dan shrugged. "Maybe. That flash of light went through her arm too."

"So she's got my skin color?" Kayla studied her hand as she wiped the tears.

"There's only one way to find out. Get dressed and we'll go to their cabin."

"Shouldn't we call first?"

"And tell them what?"

"You're right." Kayla scooped up the crystal, which was now a pale pink. "I'm bringing this too," she said as she wrapped the stone in a plastic bag and placed it in her pocketbook. "Whatever it did to me last night, it better undo today."

Kayla wore sunglasses and one of Dan's visors as the two of them rode the elevator up to the Singleton's deck. When they reached Room S1065, Dan knocked on the door.

"What is it?" a man's sleepy voice called.

"Omar," Dan said, leaning against the door and trying not to yell. "It's me and Kayla. I know it's early and we're sorry to bother you, but please open the door."

"We're not even dressed. Give us ten minutes and then come

back."

"I think you should open the door right now," Dan insisted. "Take a look at Kayla." He pushed his wife in front of the peephole.

"What the hell!" Omar shouted. Then he flung open the cabin door and stood there in his striped blue pajamas, gaping at Kayla.

"That's why we're here," Dan said as he and Kayla entered the cabin while Omar quickly shut the door.

"Where's Lisette?" Dan asked, noticing the empty bed.

"She must have gone to..." Omar's explanation was interrupted by a woman's shriek from the closed bathroom.

Seconds later, Lisette ran from the bathroom, wearing just a long Elmo tee shirt over her white legs. Her pale hands grasped her slightly sunburned face as she stared at Kayla, who had taken off the glasses and cap. "What's happened to us?"

"It must have been the crystal," Kayla said, opening her pocketbook and removing the stone, which now radiated an emerald light. "Let me try to hand it to you again."

Lisette sat on the bed and took the crystal. Nothing happened.

"You didn't change colors immediately yesterday," Omar pointed out. "It took hours."

"But there was a sudden flash," Kayla said. "Something different happened last night."

Lisette examined the rectangular stone, turning it upside down. "Yes," she agreed. "And it was red then, not green, so maybe it has to be red for us to change back."

"So how do we get this thing to turn red?" Dan asked, jabbing at the crystal.

"I don't know," Kayla said, shrugging. "It changes colors all the time. I guess we just have to watch and wait."

For the next several minutes, the two couples sat on the Singleton's bed, no one talking.

"What if we can't change back?" Kayla whispered.

"You mean stay like this?" Lisette's eyes widened.

Omar grabbed his wife's pale hand and stroked it. "I'm sure the stone will turn red again, Lis," he said.

"What are we supposed to do until it does?" Lisette asked, staring at her fingers. "I can't walk around looking like this."

"Me too," Kayla agreed.

"The ship's docked at Saint Thomas today," Dan said. "I thought we were all going shopping together after breakfast."

"But what if someone notices me?" Kayla asked.

"Cover yourself up with long sleeves, a hat, sunglasses..." Dan began.

"It's going to be ninety degrees out there!" Kayla shouted.

Her husband shrugged. "Do you want to spend today staying in the room and hiding? And what about tomorrow? We don't know how long it'll be before your skin is back to normal."

"I have an idea," Lisette whispered. "At least for the times when we're out in public."

The Godfreys and Singletons ate breakfast together, both women wearing long sleeves, jeans, and sunglasses. However, none of the passengers or crew paid extra attention to them.

Lisette's plan was for the four of them to travel as an entity so people would assume they were a black couple and a white couple—and not question who belonged with whom.

"Only the housekeeping staff really knows what we look like," Lisette had explained. "Kayla and I can try to hide from the stewards—unless you think the two of us should switch rooms till we change back." She looked at the black woman opposite.

"No," Kayla had said, shaking her light brown hair, which, like Lisette's thick black curls, hadn't been altered. "I'll just keep out of Carlo's sight."

Later that morning, the four of them left the ship together. They had feared disembarking since every passenger had to present a ship's photo ID, issued at the start of the cruise. But the crewmember manning the exit had given the women's cards a cursory glance before running them through the scanner and waving them all forward.

So now they headed to the island shops, just four vacationers: two white and two black. Although the women still wore sunglasses, they had changed into summer clothing.

"We may as well be comfortable since we can't really hide our skin color anyway," Lisette had said. She had tucked her thick dark hair into a bun, creating a sharp contrast against her pale white skin. "I guess I need suntan lotion now."

Kayla had handed her a tube of SPF 30.

When the foursome reached the first group of stores, Kayla, as she had been doing all morning, opened her purse to check the crystal's latest color. However, it still wasn't bright red; this time it was turquoise.

As the morning wore on, the temperature in St. Thomas steadily rose. By noon, the four vacationers, sweaty and exhausted, were ready to return to the ship. Carrying their bottles of liquor and assorted island souvenirs, they trudged to the dock and took out their IDs.

Again all four boarded the ship together. But, this time, the woman crewmember posted at the entrance frowned as she examined Lisette's card. "This picture not look like you," she said, staring at the woman's pale skin.

"It's me all right," Lisette said, smiling. "See my hair?" She undid the heavy bun so her black curls more closely resembled the hairdo in the photo.

"The skin?" the woman continued.

"I've been a little sick," Lisette said with a shrug. "I ate something yesterday that made my skin change color."

The crewmember shook her head. Then, hearing noise on the

gangplank, she glanced at the long line that had formed behind the foursome. "Go!" she ordered, waving them forward and hardly looking at the other three IDs as she inserted their cards into the scanner.

"Do we have to stay on board and not get off the ship tomorrow in Saint Maarten?" Lisette asked as the two couples lunched together at the pool deck's buffet.

Omar shrugged. "Maybe we should stay here. What if we get some hard-ass who won't let the two of you get back on the ship?"

Kayla opened her purse again and peeked at the crystal. "It's yellow now. It hasn't been red since last night." Her eyes widened as she looked up. "What if it never turns red again?"

"You can't think like that," Lisette said. "It hasn't even been twenty-four hours."

"Maybe we have to be proactive," Dan suggested.

"How?" Omar asked.

"Put the crystal in the water or expose it to sunlight—do something to make it change back to red."

"Forget the sunlight and water ideas," Kayla said. "It turned red in the dining room, not in the sun or water."

"So maybe leave it out on the table here and see if it turns red again," Lisette said.

"I guess it can't hurt," Kayla said. She removed the crystal from her bag and placed it on the table.

"See," Dan said, pointing to the stone. "The color's already different."

"Yeah," Omar agreed. "But it's green, not red."

"That's something," Dan said.

The foursome finished their lunch and watched the crystal. It changed color once more, becoming an eggshell blue. But it didn't turn red.

After reviewing their plans for the rest of the afternoon, the two couples parted, agreeing to meet again for dinner—unless the crystal turned red. Then Kayla would immediately get Lisette.

"I'll be easy to find," Lisette had promised. "I'm just going to sit by the pool and read."

"Don't forget the lotion," Kayla had reminded her. "My skin burns easily."

Lisette had smiled and nodded.

When Kayla and Dan returned to their cabin, Kayla removed the crystal and placed it on top of the dresser. This time it was a dark purple.

"At least that's closer to red," Dan said.

"I don't think close is good enough."

"Hand me the stone and we'll see."

"Why? If it works, you'll get Lisette's black skin."

"But you said it won't work."

"Fine." Kayla gave the crystal to Dan and the two of them felt heat radiating through the stone as the color glowed much brighter.

"I think it's happening again!" Kayla shouted. "Let go!" She pushed Dan's hand away and looked at her husband. He was now a black man.

Kayla turned towards the mirror above the dresser. Her skin was no longer Lisette's dark color. She now had Dan's tanned white skin.

"How come it changed our colors so fast?" Kayla asked.

"Maybe we held the crystal longer." Dan shrugged. "Who knows? That thing's unpredictable. But at least this proves we can change back and it doesn't just happen with red." He checked his black arms. "How do I look?"

"Like a young Denzel Washington." Kayla kissed him gently on his dark cheek. "Come on. Let's go find Lisette and Omar before something else happens."

"Oh, no!" Lisette groaned, lowering her paperback as she stared at Kayla and Dan.

"The crystal was dark purple," Kayla explained, nodding at her husband. "It was his brilliant idea to try holding it."

"At least now we know that it changes people's skins when it's another color, not just red," Dan pointed out. "And it worked fast."

"What color is the crystal now?" Lisette asked, glancing at Kayla's bag.

Kayla opened her pocketbook and peeked inside. "A soft shade of yellow. I don't think that'll work."

"Maybe we should just sit together in one of our rooms and keep trying all the crystal's colors," Lisette suggested.

"Not all," Dan said. "Just the bright dark ones."

Lisette swooped up her towel and reached for her beach bag. "Omar's relaxing in the room," she said. "Let's head there."

"What happened to you?" Omar asked as Dan entered the cabin with Lisette and Kayla. "You decided to try livin' in my skin?" He shook his head. "Well, then you better be ready to be stopped by the po-lice."

"That's not funny," Lisette said. "Dan found out the crystal also does its thing when it's purple so we all came back here to be together when it changes colors."

"Count me out," Omar said, smiling as he glanced at the other three. "I seem to be the only one who's still got the skin I was born with. The rest of you can sit together and join hands, sing 'Kumbaya,' and meditate."

"He's right," Kayla said, taking the crystal out of her handbag and placing the now pale pink stone on top of the chest of drawers. "How should we do this?"

Lisette nodded to Dan. "He's got my skin so I have to hold his hand."

"But I've got Dan's skin and you've got mine," Kayla complained.

"What about me?"

"If the three of us hold hands, we don't know whose skin we'll wind up with," Lisette said. "We have to do this just two at a time to get our original skin."

"Do you mean 'original sin'?" Omar asked, laughing.

Lisette gave her husband a friendly jab in his ribs. "Very funny."

"Look," Dan said, pointing to the crystal. "It's changing color again, getting darker." He grabbed Lisette's hand. "Come on."

Lisette picked up the crystal, which now glowed hot pink. "Do you think it's bright enough to work?" she asked.

"Who knows?" Dan said, shrugging. "But it can't hurt to try."

"Okay." Lisette thrust the crystal towards Dan, who placed his hands next to hers.

The white woman and black man stood together, their fingers wrapped around the stone.

"I don't see any flash of light," Omar said.

"Me neither," Kayla said. "And you both look the same."

Lisette placed the crystal back on top of the dresser and sat on the bed. "I guess it doesn't work with pink," she said.

Omar reached into the top drawer and removed a deck of cards. "You guys want to play some poker while we wait?" he asked, shuffling the deck. "It's gonna be kind of boring just staring at the stone."

"It's getting close to dinner time," Omar said, checking his watch. "What do you all want to do?"

Kayla tossed her cards on the table and stood. "We've been here nearly two hours, tried a whole bunch of colors, and nothing's worked," she said. "Let's meet for an early dinner and keep trying." She walked to the dresser, lifted the crystal—now a smoky gray—and put it in her handbag.

"If it turns another dark color before dinner, we'll call you," Dan said to Lisette as he opened the cabin door.

"Okay, I guess," she whispered.

Omar put his dark arm around his wife's pale shoulders. "It'll be fine," he said.

"How can you be sure? It's been almost a day."

"I just know. Anyway, you're beautiful whatever color you are."

The Godfreys and Singletons once again shared a dinner table, this time as two multiracial couples. "We look so conspicuous," Lisette, a white woman sipping a glass of Chablis, whispered.

"Not really," Omar said. "People'll assume we're friends because we're both black men with white wives."

"You think anyone remembers us from last night when Lisette was black and Dan was white?" Kayla asked, lowering her wine glass.

Omar shook his head. "Nah. It's a big dining room and we're on the opposite side with different waiters."

"And the crew sees so many passengers, we must all look alike to them anyway," Dan added.

"You're probably right," Kayla said, turning her attention to the pale green crystal in the center of the table as she finished her wine. "It's not turning dark colors any more."

"Give it a chance," Dan said. "It's only been a couple of hours."

During the lengthy dinner, Dan and Lisette tried holding the crystal twice—once when it was a fairly bright yellow and another time when it was a shade of burnt orange. But no sparks radiated and their skins didn't change colors.

Afterwards, the two couples sat in one of the ship's hallway lounges to decide what to do next.

"We should stop thinking about the crystal all the time and go to the comedy show for some laughs," Omar suggested.

"That's easy for you to say," Lisette said. "Your skin's the same."

"Omar's right," Dan said. "If we just relax tonight, the crystal might turn red or purple again. Maybe its colors have something to do with our feelings."

"No way!" Kayla shouted. "We weren't feeling anything special when Lisette and I touched it last night."

"But the stone's different now," Omar explained. "This afternoon, you and Dan changed skin colors immediately."

Lisette nodded. "The man does have a point," she said. "We'll sit together and leave the crystal on the table so we can check it." She rose to her feet. "Let's watch the comedian. Omar's right about that too. We can sure use a good laugh."

They found a table for four in the large lounge where white-haired comic, Sy Samuels, was performing. After ordering drinks, they all sipped their cocktails and waited for the show to begin.

"He's so old," Kayla whispered as the elderly man walked gingerly to the stage and grabbed the microphone. "He doesn't look like he's any good. He doesn't even look like he can stand up long enough to finish his act."

"You're wrong about him," Omar said. "Sy Samuels is an old-timer, but he's really funny. Just wait."

The two couples watched and listened as the comic, in a surprisingly strong voice, delivered a non-stop barrage of one-liners. Soon they were all laughing hysterically.

"I can't believe he's this good," Kayla said, wiping away her tears during the comedian's short break, which allowed the patrons to order additional drinks.

"I told you," Omar said. "I've seen Sy Samuels before. He used to be on late night TV—Leno and Letterman, I think."

"Too bad the crystal doesn't seem to like him much." Kayla pointed to the beige stone as she sipped her third bourbon. "It hasn't turned any bright colors since we sat down."

"Shh," Dan said. "He's starting again. Just enjoy the show."

When the comic finished his performance, both couples—along

with the rest of the audience—gave him a standing ovation.

"Great idea!" Kayla said to Omar, slurring her words. "I'm so glad we came here." As she reached for the pale pink crystal, Kayla felt woozy and stumbled forward. Her knees hit the small table, knocking it over and sending cocktail glasses and the crystal crashing onto the polished wooden floor—everything shattering into tiny pieces.

The Godfreys and Singletons stared silently at the remnants of the crystal, now just ordinary slivers of smoky gray stone.

"I'm so sorry," Kayla whispered.

Lisette rubbed her white arm. "Does this mean...?" she asked, her voice trailing off.

"Yes," Dan said, a frown forming on his dark face. "These are now our permanent skins."

THE PLANT WHISPERER

I really love my job. Why? Because it's mostly stress-free. Take it from someone who knows. I used to be an inner-city schoolteacher, which gave me a case of hives that lasted the entire school year.

So when Vicki Tomiselli told me her company was looking for someone to take care of their indoor plants, I realized it was the perfect job for me. First of all, I love gardening. Second of all, plants aren't like people; they don't talk back to you. At least, that's what I thought.

In September, I became a professional plant caretaker. Since then, I've lined up more than twenty downtown office buildings as clients, which keeps me pretty busy. And, until a couple of weeks ago, I'd been stress-free—and also hive-free.

But all that changed on a Tuesday afternoon when I went into the lobby of Kensico Investments to prune and water their hanging ivy baskets. I stood on the stepladder and snipped a dead leaf, accidentally destroying a neighboring bit of foliage.

"Watch out!" a haughty British man's voice warned.

I looked around the lobby. It was empty, except for the guard sleeping in one of the chairs and the receptionist in the far left corner, her eyes focused on her cellphone.

"Who said that?" I asked.

"I did."

I looked again and still saw no one.

"Dummy! You're staring right at me."

"The English ivy?" I whispered.

"Yes, of course that's me. Who else did you hurt just now? That leaf was perfectly fine until you murdered it."

"I'm sorry." *What else could I say?*

"Just don't do it again."

"I won't...When did you learn to talk?"

"I always knew how to talk, just never had a reason to."

"And now you have a reason?"

"Yes."

I waited for an explanation. When nothing was forthcoming, I prodded. "So..."

"So I heard something yesterday."

"And..."

"Shut up and let me finish! As I started to say, a man and a woman came in here and stood under me, talking quietly to themselves. They were looking at the building, making notes."

As I listened, I watered the talking plant.

"Not too much," the English ivy ordered. "Last time you overwatered me."

Just what I need—a talking plant with an attitude! "Sorry," I apologized. "But what you said doesn't sound very important."

"That's what you think, smarty girl. What if I told you those two used the word 'robbery'?"

I lifted the watering can and stared at the ivy plant.

"You're sure?" I asked.

"I swear on all my leaves."

I stayed on the ladder, hoping the receptionist wouldn't look up from her phone and wonder why I was still watering the same plant. But she was busy texting.

"What else did the people say?" I asked.

"They said this was a good building to rob because there was only one guard who wasn't any good."

They were right. The guy always fell asleep in one of the lobby chairs. Maybe he had a night job.

"Can you describe what the people looked like?"

"I already told you: One was a man and the other was a woman."

"But what did they look like? Were they tall or short? What color was their skin and their hair?"

"I don't know. All you people look the same to me."

"Did they say when they were going to commit the robbery?"

"No."

I shook my head. "I don't have enough information to give the company or the police," I told the plant as I stepped down from the ladder. "Thanks, anyway."

I finished watering the rest of the plants in Kensico Investments without any other interruptions. By that I mean none of the other plants talked to me.

At work in the other office buildings, I thought about my weird conversation with the hanging ivy plant. It made no sense: a plant talking to me about a robbery. By the time I got home, I had convinced myself that I'd imagined the whole thing. I talked to plants all the time when I watered them so I must have wanted the ivy to say something back. I had probably been especially tired too.

When I returned to Kensico Investments the following Tuesday, I had totally dismissed the incident. But I couldn't resist saying something to the "talking" plant. "Good morning," I said. "Got any more news for me?"

"The man and woman came here again," the ivy said in its British accent.

I almost fell off the ladder. "So it did happen," I whispered.

"You really can talk."

"God!" the plant groaned. "I thought we had gotten past this."

I checked the receptionist. She was joking with the mailman, who was young and cute and didn't seem to be in any hurry to deliver the rest of his mail.

"When did the two of them come in?" I asked the plant.

"Yesterday."

"Did they say anything new about the robbery?"

"Yes."

"What did they say?"

"If I tell you, what's in it for me?"

A plant shakedown?

"What do you want?"

"More sunlight. Move me closer to the windows."

"You want me to switch you with the fat Irish ivy?"

"Yeah. Colleen's fat because she gets all that extra sun. Move me and I'll tell you what they said."

The receptionist and the mailman were still busy chatting. He had tossed his bag of letters on the floor and now leaned against her desk, whispering sweet somethings. The only other person in the lobby was the guard, asleep in a chair near the entrance.

Quickly, I switched the two plants and moved next to the window to resume the conversation.

"So as you were saying..." I began.

"They said they would do the job next week, probably Thursday, if Frank could be there then."

"Who's Frank?"

"How the hell would I know?"

"Did the woman call the man 'Frank'?"

"No."

"Did she call him another name?"

"Yeah. She poked him and said he was a 'big dummy.'"

"Then Frank must be someone else."

"Obviously."

"What about the woman? Did the big dummy call her by name?"

"He called her 'Rita.'"

Rita, big dummy, and Frank...not much to go by.

"Can you tell me what the man and woman look like?"

"Big dummy is big and fat like Colleen. Rita is small and thin like Sven over there."

"You mean that scrawny Swedish ivy."

"Yeah. I think you forgot to water him a couple of times."

"No, I didn't."

"Well, that's what she looks like."

"Do all the plants here have names?"

"Of course we do."

"What's your name?"

"Archibald, but you can call me Archie."

"Thanks for the information, Archie," I said. "My name's Alicia and I'll do my best to stop the robbery."

"What do you mean you heard two people planning a robbery?" Fiona Sheppard, VP of Kensico Investments, asked me as I stood in front of her desk.

"I was watering the plants today and this couple was talking quietly nearby," I explained.

"Why didn't you tell the guard so he could have questioned them?"

"It happened so fast that, by the time I turned around to get him, they were already gone."

"Did you get a look at them?"

"Not really because I was standing on top of the ladder. I just know it was a big beefy guy and a small woman."

"And you're sure you heard them say they planned to rob us on Thursday?"

"Yes, but they weren't sure of the day because they said they needed another guy named Frank."

Fiona Sheppard picked up a pen from her neat desk and twirled it with her fingers. She was a pretty blonde in her late forties, maybe older, who always looked perfectly put together. I wish I could tame my hair like that.

"I don't think I can act on this," she said. "You've given me so little information—and you're not even sure of the day this robbery is supposed to happen."

"Can't you at least get another guard?"

"Why? What's wrong with Wilbur?"

I didn't want to rat out the sleeping guard. "Nothing's wrong with him," I said. "But they're expecting just one guard to be here so having two guards might be enough to stop the robbery."

"I'll discuss it with the board and alert Wilbur and the police," she said. "Thanks for your help, Alicia, and let me know if you see those two in here again."

I didn't return to Kensico Investments until the following Wednesday. This time a couple of people were standing near the lobby entrance, and, of course, Wilbur was there too, sacked out in one of the chairs.

I moved my stepladder and watering can next to the window where Archie, the talking English ivy, hung in the bright sunlight. "How's everything?" I asked quietly.

"Lousy," he muttered.

"Why? You're in the sun, where you wanted to be."

"Yes, but it gets too hot."

I shook my head. "You can't have it both ways."

"Shut up and just give me extra water. I'm as parched as a desert cactus."

I watered him and didn't say anything else.

"That's better. I'm sorry if I'm a bit grumpy, but I was really thirsty and you're a day late."

"I had a dentist appointment." *Now I'm making excuses to a plant.*

"They came in again yesterday. If you were here when you should have been, you would have seen them."

"The man and the woman?"

"No, the man in the moon."

A snooty, sarcastic plant.

"Did they say anything new?"

"They're on for Thursday because Frank will be able to help them."

"I told the vice president about it last week."

"I know. She spoke to Wilbur."

"Are they getting an extra guard? I suggested that."

"No, just Wilbur."

"Really?"

"She told Wilbur that the company trusted him to handle any problem that developed."

"What about the police?"

"She didn't say anything about the police."

"The police said they didn't have enough information to warrant assigning extra officers here," Fiona Sheppard explained when I questioned her after I'd finished watering and pruning all the ivies.

"Not even a patrol car in front of the building to maybe scare them off?"

Miss Perfect shrugged. "With the city's current financial crisis, there's no extra money. Besides, you said the man and woman weren't even sure they would do anything tomorrow."

I couldn't tell her Frank was available so the robbery was definitely on for Thursday. *How would I know that?* "But, but..." I stammered.

Fiona Sheppard rose from her swivel chair, her navy pantsuit wrinkle-free. "Thank you for your concern, Alicia," she said. "I've informed the police, I've alerted Wilbur, and that's all I can do. We will be extra vigilant tomorrow and if any visitors look suspicious..." Her voice trailed off as she walked to the door of her office and ushered me out.

It wasn't my problem if Kensico Investments got robbed. I wasn't even an employee of the company; I just took care of their plants. Still, the situation bothered me.

For the rest of the day, I couldn't stop thinking about the two robbers and Frank. I was curious: How were they going to pull off the robbery?

Thursday morning, I called in sick to my other office buildings, saying I'd be there Friday. Then I tucked my unruly brown hair into a Cincinnati Reds baseball cap and added a pair of rhinestone-trimmed sunglasses, a baggy gray sweatshirt, and old faded jeans. Hoping no one would recognize me, I hopped into the car and drove to Kensico Investments.

After parking in the nearby lot, I wasn't sure what to do next. *Should I go inside and just sit and wait?* They didn't have many visitors and I didn't know when the robbery would happen so I couldn't stay there all day. Even if Wilbur didn't notice me, someone else would. Finally, I had an idea.

I entered the building, walked to the window, and stood under the English ivy.

"Archie," I whispered, not wanting to wake the sleeping guard, passed out in a chair near me.

"What are you wearing?" the plant asked. He sounded horrified.

"I'm disguised."

"But you look dreadful. Couldn't you find a more attractive costume?"

"I don't want anyone here to notice me. I'm going to try to stop the robbery."

"If you're a hero, do you want someone to photograph you

looking like that?"

Not wanting to argue, I initiated my plan. I took out my phone and pretended to make a call. "Helen," I said to an imaginary person. "I'm at Kensico like we agreed. Where are you?" I paused for effect. "What?" I acted surprised. "You haven't even left the house yet?" I checked my watch. "Okay, I'll wait. But get here as soon as you can."

I must have been a little too dramatic because Wilbur opened his eyes and looked at me. For a second I thought he might see through my disguise, but his sleepy expression didn't change.

I smiled sweetly and took a step towards him. "I'm meeting a friend," I explained. "But she's gonna be late."

He nodded and closed his eyes again.

I found a seat near Archie, returned to the phone and made believe I was fiddling with it. But my attention was focused on the entrance. "Tell me if the robbers come in," I whispered.

"At least you could have chosen a more attractive hat," the plant muttered.

After thirty minutes, I again phoned my imaginary friend. "Your car broke down?" I said. "Geez!"

Pretending to be very upset, I jumped out of the chair and left the building. Then I leaned against the wall and stared at the street, trying to come up with another plan—some other reason to be inside.

That's when I saw a big fat guy, a short woman, and a skinny man crossing the road and heading for Kensico Investments. I dashed back into the building and stood under Archie. "I think they're coming," I whispered.

"Brilliant deduction," the plant said in its haughty British accent. "You should have been a police officer."

The trio entered the lobby and approached the receptionist. The heavyset guy and the girl said something to her.

"What are they saying?" I asked Archie.

"How should I know? I don't have super-hearing."

After their brief conversation, the robbers took seats nearby, giving me a chance to study them. They didn't look at all threatening.

The woman was young, maybe in her mid-twenties, with long hair in a ponytail. She wore black slacks and a silky black-and-white striped shirt. The men, both in their early forties, each wore dark suits and ties. The fat guy's suit was a little too tight, but otherwise he looked good. In fact, they all looked good. *Did robbers dress up for a robbery?*

I glanced in Wilbur's direction. The guard was still sleeping in the chair.

Five minutes later, I saw Fiona Sheppard heading towards the trio. I lowered my head and listened.

"Good morning," she said. "You wanted to discuss some possible investments?"

"Yes," the beefy guy said. "We've come into some money."

"Let's go into my office and talk," Fiona said.

I heard the three of them get up and follow her.

"Archie," I whispered. "Why didn't Fiona Sheppard recognize the robbers? I described them to her yesterday."

"People are stupid. I can't explain your species."

"She actually invited them into her office. What can I do?"

"How should I know? I'm just a plant, remember?"

"I have to do something," I said. "I'm going to wake Wilbur."

"That's your solution?"

"I don't have any other way of getting into Fiona Sheppard's office. I need somebody with a swipe card."

"Good luck."

I rushed to the snoozing guard. "Wilbur," I said. "Wake up. I need your help."

He continued to snore softly.

"Please," I said louder. "Wake up!"

Still I got no reaction.

I grabbed the guard's shoulders and shook them. "Get up, now!" I yelled.

"Huh?" The man opened his eyes, blinked twice, and stared at me. "What's wrong?" he asked.

"Everything," I said. "I need to go to Fiona Sheppard's office right now. I think she's being robbed."

"Do I know you? You look familiar."

"We'll talk later. Right now, I have to get to her office."

I grabbed Wilbur's hand and practically shoved him out of the chair. "Come on," I said. "Let's go."

Wilbur used his badge to get from the lobby to the inner offices. Since I had been in Fiona Sheppard's office twice recently, I already knew the location.

"Faster," I said.

"Why are we here again?" he asked.

Duh! "Miss Sheppard's with some people who might be robbing her."

"Like a stick-up?"

"Yes."

"I hope I remembered the gun." He patted his holster. "Yup, I got it."

Somehow, Wilbur didn't inspire me with great confidence.

We reached the closed door of Fiona Sheppard's office and I heard voices inside.

"What do we do now?" the guard asked. "Want me to knock down the door?"

Now he was really into it!

"Let's just listen first," I suggested.

The conversation didn't sound loud or threatening. It was mostly a man talking and I thought I recognized Fiona Sheppard's voice. But even when I put my head against the door, I couldn't understand any of the words.

Then I heard footsteps in the hallway. "Knock on the door," I ordered.

Wilbur knocked.

"What is it?" Fiona Sheppard asked without opening the door.

When Wilbur didn't answer, I poked him in the ribs. "Ask her if everything is okay," I instructed.

"Is everything okay?" the guard asked.

I heard footsteps inside and Fiona Sheppard opened the door, closing it behind her. She looked at us and frowned. "What's going on?" she asked.

"The robbery..." I began.

She squinted at me. "Alicia, is that you?"

"Yes."

"Why are you dressed like that—and why are you here?"

"Today is Thursday and those people inside your office—the man, the woman, and Frank..."

"Oh, that's right." She nodded her head. "You think they're robbers." She smiled at me. "Come in." Then she seemed to notice the guard for the first time. "You too, Wilbur."

We stepped inside the office where the three visitors sat, all with black binders resting on their laps. The woman's folder was open to a page titled, "Is Your Business Safe and Secure?"

"These people who you thought were robbing Kensico Investments," Fiona Sheppard began. "They're actually working for us, updating our security system. This is Tom McDeavitt, Rita Frye, and their boss, Frank Machessi."

"I don't understand," I said.

"You thought we were robbers?" the big guy, Tom, asked, chuckling. "We always check out the building before making our report. We try to think like robbers, pretend we're going to pull off a robbery—what would they do?"

"I better get back," Wilbur said, retreating towards the door.

"Ah, the sleeping guard," Rita said, wagging her forefinger. "We've been watching you."

Wilbur scurried away.

Tom looked at me again, this time more carefully. "We've been in this building several times, but the lobby's always been empty. How were you able to overhear us?"

"I just water the plants so maybe you didn't notice me."

"You weren't here," Rita said emphatically, pointing at me. "It's my job to be observant and I'm sure I've never seen you before—so how did you know?"

What could I say? That a plant told me? When I couldn't explain, Fiona Sheppard called the police and I was taken to the station for questioning.

Of course I didn't tell the police anything either so, after an hour, they let me go. And Kensico Investments didn't press charges. What could they have charged me with anyway? I didn't commit a crime.

But Kensico did fire me (and Wilbur too). Now I no longer talk to Archie, and, at the companies where I still work, I make sure I don't talk to—or listen to—any of the plants.

BEHIND THE FENCE

The fence had always been there. At least it had been there for Marcus' whole life—all thirteen years. The fence was just a quarter-mile from his house so he saw it nearly every day.

It was tall—more than ten feet high with barbed wire along the top. And it was long too, covering a whole block. All you could see from the outside was a field of weedy uncut grass and a few trees. The only entrance to the property was padlocked and Marcus had never seen anyone go in or out.

Nobody seemed to know what was inside the fence. Marcus had asked many people. "I heard a millionaire bought the land years ago," his mother had said.

"But why?" Marcus had prodded.

"I have no clue," his mother had said.

Others said the property belonged to a movie star or the government owned it. Marcus had even gone to town hall and asked about the fenced-in land, but the woman behind the counter wouldn't give him an answer.

"The owner doesn't want to be identified," the tall white lady with glasses had told him.

"That's allowed?" Marcus had asked.

The woman had nodded. "As long as the owner takes care of the property and pays the taxes."

"But nobody takes care of it," Marcus had argued. "The grass is never mowed so it's real high."

"There's a fence, right?"

"Yeah, a big one."

"And the property is clean, with no junk thrown or kept inside?"

"I guess."

"Then the property is considered to be well-maintained." The woman had shrugged. "I'm sorry. There's nothing else I can tell you."

Monday after school, Marcus stood near the entrance to the fence with his friend, Simon. "I'm gonna get inside," Marcus said.

"No way." Simon laughed and stared at the padlocked door. "Ain't gonna happen, man."

"Not through the gate." Marcus beckoned Simon closer and, even though no one was nearby, whispered, "I found a way to get in."

"Yeah? Where?"

"I'll show you." Marcus walked around the corner and Simon followed. Simon was a tall skinny kid with light brown skin and wavy black hair—kind of a goofball—but Marcus liked him because he was good-natured and trustworthy. He thought Simon could keep the information about the fence a secret. At least he hoped so.

Marcus reached the spot where a rabbit or some other animal had chewed a hole through the fence near the bottom. He had covered the small opening with part of an old green dishtowel. Now he removed the cloth and Simon examined the space. "No way you can fit yourself through there," his friend said, shaking his head.

Marcus bent down on his knees and lifted the fence under

the hole. "It comes up under here," he said, demonstrating the weakness. "See? If I dig a little, there'll be enough room."

He looked up at Simon. "I've got to get home and do my homework first or my mom'll be mad. But I'm coming back at five o'clock with a shovel to check what's inside here. Want to come with me?"

"Sure," Simon said.

Marcus was digging under the fence when Simon joined him. "How's it going?" Simon asked.

"What took you so long?" Marcus straightened his back and leaned against the shovel. "I could've used some help," he said. "Now I'm almost done."

"Sorry. I'll finish the job." Simon grabbed the shovel and energetically attacked the hole.

"So why weren't you here at five like you said?" Marcus asked.

"I got caught up in something."

"Not your homework, that's for sure." Simon was a smart kid, but a notoriously lazy student.

"Playing Batman Knight."

"My mom says video games will fry your brains."

"Your mom says a lot of things."

"So what?"

"So nothing...Is this big enough for you to get through?" Simon stopped digging and looked at Marcus, who was six inches shorter and just as thin.

"Yeah," Marcus said. "But I don't know if the hole's big enough for you."

Simon dropped the shovel. "I'm not going in there with you," he said.

"Why not?"

"I got things to do."

"Like playing that stupid Batman game?"

Simon turned and gave Marcus a quick wave and smile. "Have fun."

Marcus hid the shovel behind a nearby bush before squeezing his body through the opening under the fence. Once inside, he looked for something he could use to remember the location of the hole. When he noticed a large dead branch, Marcus took the stick and planted it into the ground near the fence.

Satisfied with the marker, he started walking through the heavy grass towards the middle of the property, anxious to see what was hidden behind the fence.

He walked for several minutes without seeing anything except the few trees he had already observed from the outside. Then he saw something ahead that was nearly completely hidden by the overgrown grass.

It was a building—not a house, but a small shed made of corrugated metal, a place where people stored tools or garden equipment. When Marcus reached the shed, he realized it was old and rusted and looked as if it hadn't been used for years. But, like the fence, the shed's double doors were locked. Marcus yanked on the combination lock, but it didn't open and, since there were no windows, he couldn't see what was inside.

Marcus backed away and folded his arms, staring at the old shed. After a couple of minutes, he shook his head and turned around.

Knowing something was hidden behind the fence really bothered Marcus. During school Tuesday, he couldn't concentrate at all. He kept thinking about what might be locked in that shed.

A bomb? A dead body? Stolen money? Whatever was in there wasn't tools or lawn furniture. It was something the owner didn't want discovered. Otherwise, why would the rusty old shed be locked?

How can I open it? Marcus considered some possibilities. *Pliers? A wrench? Dad must have that stuff in his toolbox.*

Bust the lock. Marcus knew that was a crime—*like breaking and entering...*

He shook his head. But this wasn't a house; it was just an old rusty shed. And maybe what was in there was something bad or dangerous. *Then everyone'll be proud and reporters'll interview me and I'll be on TV and YouTube and...*

"Marcus!"

He lifted his head and saw the angry face of Mrs. Berkowitz, his social studies teacher. "I asked you a question," she said.

"Can you please repeat it?" Marcus asked meekly as he reluctantly shoved his plan for getting into the shed to the recesses of his mind.

After school, Marcus, armed with pliers and a wrench, returned to the fence. He found the opening he had dug, now hidden with leaves, and again crawled through. Then he walked rapidly, face down, following the footprints he had left the day before by slogging through and pushing down the high grass. When his trail of footprints ended, he stopped and looked up, expecting to see the rusty shed.

But there was no building in front of him; nothing was there except a few trees and more tall grass.

Marcus backed away and frowned. Maybe he had gone the wrong way. *Followed another trail?*

He placed his left foot into one of the impressions in the grass and it was exactly the same size. Those were his footprints. *So where'd the shed go?* It couldn't have just disappeared.

"I didn't imagine it," Marcus muttered to himself. "It was right here yesterday."

Marcus sat in the grass for several minutes, unsure of what to do next. He couldn't very well complain to anyone about the missing shed since he wasn't supposed to be inside the fence.

Maybe something else's here.

Marcus walked further into the property. He trudged past a small bush and a straggly tree until he came to an area with shorter grass that looked like it had been mowed a few weeks ago. He continued through the low grass until he reached a green rectangle that was screwed into the ground.

The rectangle wasn't very large—about two feet long and eighteen inches wide—and it seemed to be made of metal because, when Marcus tapped it, the piece made a clangy echoing noise. He tried to lift the rectangle, but it didn't budge.

Marcus reached into his pocket and took out the pliers and wrench he had expected to use to open the shed's lock. He tried both tools, hoping to loosen the four screws. Neither worked. Then he attempted to pry apart the metal, first with the wrench and then the pliers. But again the rectangle didn't move.

"I need a screwdriver," he said out loud. But there was no time to get the tool, climb back inside the fence, and open the screws of the rectangle wedged into the ground. His mom would be home soon.

Tomorrow. I'll do it tomorrow.

Wednesday afternoon Marcus returned to the fence, this time armed with a screwdriver. After he climbed through the bottom opening, he followed the trail he had made in the tall grass to the spot with the green rectangle. But along the way, he saw something that made him stop and gawk.

The rusty shed was back—just where it had been two days ago.

Marcus walked up to the small building and tapped the metal. It was real. *It's here. I'm not making this up.*

The shed was still locked—and Marcus no longer carried a wrench or pliers, just a screwdriver. He tugged at the lock, but it still didn't open. Shaking his head, Marcus found the path he had made by trampling the grass the day before and continued along the trail.

When he reached the shorter grass, Marcus walked to the spot with the rectangle. He found it, except now the rectangle was just an impression in the grass—the same size as the green piece of metal he had seen. Only there was no metal in the ground anymore.

Marcus sat and stared at the outline, totally confused. *What's going on here?*

In school the next day, Marcus cornered Simon after English class. "I need you to go behind the fence with me," Marcus said as they headed to the gym.

"Why?"

"I'm seeing strange stuff inside there."

"Like what?"

"I can't explain. I gotta show you."

Simon stopped walking and studied Marcus. "Is it scary?' he asked.

"No, just weird."

"You sure?"

"Simon, please! I really need you to see this. It's not dangerous or scary—I promise."

Simon sighed and rolled his eyes dramatically. "Okay, I'll go."

"Thanks, man." Marcus slapped his friend's shoulder. "Meet me at the gate at four."

Marcus let out a long breath as he reached the entrance to the fence. "I was afraid you wouldn't show," he said to Simon.

"Promised I'd be here. You got me kinda curious about what's inside."

"This way," Marcus said, motioning towards the part of the fence with the hole on the bottom. "I made it bigger last time so you can fit."

"You didn't even know I'd come."

Marcus smiled. "I hoped you would."

After the boys crawled through the opening and camouflaged it with leaves, Marcus led Simon towards the rusty shed. "Let's see if it's here this time," he murmured.

"If what's here?"

"It was here, then it was gone, and then it was here again."

"Huh?"

"See these footprints?" Marcus asked as they trudged through the tall grass. "I made them."

"So?"

"So this is where I saw it."

"Saw what?" Simon shouted.

"Shh."

"Why do I have to be quiet? There's no one else here."

"Still, there's strange shit going on."

The boys reached the spot where the shed had been.

"Damn!" Marcus muttered. "It's gone again."

"You're not making any sense," Simon complained. "There's nothing here."

Marcus pointed to the grass. "See those lines in the ground? That's where the shed was."

"There's no shed."

"Not now, but it was here yesterday."

"Oh yeah? Then where'd it go?"

Marcus shrugged. "That's what's so weird. I have no clue. It was here Monday when I went through the fence—the day you left. Then when I came back Tuesday, it was gone—and yesterday, it was here again."

"That's crazy. A building can't do that."

"I know," Marcus agreed. "But this building can."

"I found something else," Marcus said as he and Simon continued slogging through the tall grass.

"Something else that disappeared?"

"Yeah."

"What'd you find?"

"Let's see if it's still here first. Then I can just show you 'cause I don't really know what it is."

Marcus and Simon reached the area with the short grass. "It was right over there," Marcus said, running ahead.

"There's nothing here," Simon said when he joined Marcus.

"But you can see where it was." Marcus pointed to the outline of a rectangle in the grass. "It was made of green metal and screwed into the ground." He removed a screwdriver from his jeans pocket. "That's why I took this—to open it and find out what was underneath."

"It's just grass."

"Today, but not that other time."

Simon rubbed his skinny arms. "All this shit about things disappearing is creepy," he said. "Let's get out of here."

"No," Marcus said. "Not yet. We're already inside the fence so we gotta check out everything." He pointed to the tall grass on the left. "I want to go that way."

The grass on the left seemed even higher and thicker to Marcus.

"Ow!" Simon shouted as he reached down to massage his left ankle. "Something just bit me!"

"Keep it down," Marcus whispered.

"I wanna get outta here!"

"Don't be a baby. There's gotta be something else...Look!" Marcus waved his arms. "Do you see that?"

"No."

"It's some kind of circle thing."

"Big deal."

Marcus ran towards a clear structure that was mostly hidden by the grass.

"So what is it?" Simon asked when he caught up to Marcus.

"I don't know," Marcus said. He walked to the eight-foot semicircle wedged into the ground and tapped it. "Feels like plastic, but it's not hot from the sun."

"It's nothing." Simon turned and headed in the opposite direction. "Just a big dumb piece of plastic and now we gotta walk all the way back to get outta here."

"Simon!" Marcus called. "Something's happening!"

Simon ran to where Marcus stood and, as the two boys watched, the semicircular object began vibrating. The ground beneath them shook too.

"I wanna go home," Simon whined.

"No." Marcus grabbed his friend's hand and guided Simon a few feet away from the shaking semicircle. "We have to see this."

"Why?"

"Cause..." Before Marcus could explain his reasons—which he wasn't sure of anyway—the rest of the semicircle broke through the ground.

"Half of it was buried," Marcus said, looking at the whirling sphere that now rotated in place on the flattened grass, much like a huge globe.

"What is it?" Simon whispered.

"I don't know, but it's way cool. Look at all the colors." Even though the sphere was transparent, the sun's rays created a prism effect of red, green, yellow, and blue flashes.

Marcus stood transfixed, watching the light show. "Man, this is great!" he said.

"You must leave," a raspy voice ordered. To Marcus, the words sounded mechanical, like a talking robot.

"Who said that?" Simon asked as he clutched Marcus' tee shirt.

"It's coming from inside the ball," Marcus whispered. "Who are you?" he shouted. "And what are you doing here?"

"You must leave," the voice repeated. "You must leave now."

"C'mon," Simon said, pulling his friend's arm. "You heard that."

"Did you do all that stuff—making things disappear?" Marcus asked.

The ground shuddered again and the earth separated, a large fissure forming between the sphere and the boys.

"Go!" the raspy voice shouted.

As the ground beneath them continued to throb more violently, Marcus reluctantly followed Simon away from the globe. When the ground stopped shaking, he turned to stare at the sphere, but it was no longer there. All Marcus could see was the flattened grass and the many newly-formed gaps in the earth.

Marcus returned to the fence by himself after school Friday and retraced his steps. The imprints of the shed and rectangle were still there along with the crevices where the ground had separated, but none of the objects remained—no shed, no green rectangle, and no spinning globe.

He tried to talk about the experience with Simon, but his friend refused to discuss it. "Way too weird, man," Simon said. "Forget about it."

But Marcus couldn't forget. He thought about what happened behind the fence all the time. The shed had disappeared and come back. He figured whatever was in the globe was still hiding there and would return too. *I'll find it*, Marcus promised himself. *I'll never give up.*

LOCAL BOY MISSING!

LARKWOOD – Thirteen-year-old Marcus Montgomery, a seventh-grader from Kensington Middle School, disappeared two days ago. According to the boy's mother, Antonia Montgomery, 39, Marcus went outside to play Saturday morning and never returned home.

Simon Freaton, 13, told authorities that his friend liked to explore a nearby gated and fenced property. Police searched the large empty lot, but found no trace of the boy.

Sergeant Tom Kincaid asked residents with any leads to contact the police department. "We're totally stumped," he admitted.

NATHAN'S RETURN

Isabel was sitting in Carly's Coffee Shoppe, nibbling a bran muffin and skimming the *Daily Herald*, when she saw him. She dropped the food and clutched the table tightly with both arms.

"No," she whispered. "It can't be him."

Of course, it's not, she realized when she got a better view of the man across the street getting into the red sports car. Nathan had gone missing many years ago and this man was in his late forties, about the same age Nathan had been then.

But he looks so much like Nathan. Isabel picked up the muffin and took a bite as she watched the car speed away. *That car*...Nathan had loved shiny red sports cars. He would have been driving a car like that.

She let out a deep sigh. *Why now?* She hadn't thought about her missing husband for a long time as she struggled to get on with her life. Then she glanced at the newspaper on the table and noticed the date—May 6th. Now it all made sense. Today was the twenty-fifth anniversary of Nathan's disappearance.

It had been a mild spring day—sunny and comfortably warm. Nathan, a real estate broker, had been at work, and she had been working too, in her home office, proofing a tech manual.

The weather had been so delightful that Isabel had taken time off in the afternoon to walk around the block and then sit outside. Maybe she had even taken a short nap on the front porch rocking chair, or maybe she'd just been daydreaming. She wasn't quite sure.

In any case, that's where she had been sitting when she'd gotten the phone call. She remembered the conversation vividly.

"Isabel!" Maude, the receptionist at Dunham Realty, had shouted.

"What's wrong?" Isabel had asked.

"Do you know where Nathan is?"

"No...Isn't he there?"

"He had an appointment at two. He was supposed to meet a couple at the Richardson house, but he never showed."

Isabel had looked at her watch and realized it was after four o'clock. "Where could he be?" she had mumbled.

"It's not like him at all," Maude had continued. "He knew those people were buying the house. They just wanted to see it one more time before signing the contract. You're sure you don't know where Nathan is?"

"No," she had whispered. "I have no idea."

And the police hadn't known either. Isabel had told them Nathan had driven to work that morning and that was the last time she had seen him.

Maude had confirmed Nathan had been at the office in the morning, left for lunch, and never returned. Poof! Nathan had just vanished; one day he had been there and then he was gone.

And now, for the first time in twenty-five years, Isabel had seen someone who looked like Nathan—the Nathan who had disappeared.

Isabel tried to shove her memories of Nathan to the back of her head as she drove home, to the same Colonial house she had shared with her husband.

She unlocked the front door and stepped inside. Then she smiled—something Isabel did nearly every time she entered the house. It was so warm and inviting, decorated just the way she liked—very contemporary.

When Nathan lived with her, he had lobbied for ornate furnishings, the kind French kings preferred. Since Isabel hated all the heavy wood and intricate patterns, they had compromised: rococo bedroom, modern living room, French dining room, contemporary rec room, and so on.

Isabel shook her head as she leaned against the door. The furniture mishmash had never really worked; the styles were too diverse. Then, after Nathan disappeared, she had redecorated—and now the house looked wonderful.

Isabel still proofread tech materials, only now all her work was done online. After her visit to the coffee shop, she sat in a backyard lounge chair with her laptop.

Like the day twenty-five years earlier, May 6th was gorgeous and Isabel was having trouble focusing on her task. Every few minutes, she lost concentration and found herself staring at the sky or the birds or the trees—at anything but the "Build Your Own Kitchen" guide she was supposed to be proofing.

She turned away from the laptop once more and glanced at the road. A red sports car was parked across the street.

Isabel jumped up, nearly knocking over the computer as she rushed to the car. When she reached the road, she realized it was the same car she had seen earlier—and the man behind the wheel was the same Nathan look-alike.

This time, Isabel was determined to remember the make of the car and the license plate number. It was an Acura and the license plate was V6X4258. She repeated the numbers in her head while continuing to stare at the driver, who clutched the steering wheel and faced the road, not paying any attention to her.

"Nathan?" Isabel asked as she crossed the street. She knew it was foolish to call her husband's name, but the resemblance was so striking that she couldn't help herself.

Isabel was just two feet from the car when the driver sped away. She looked at the fading license plate, repeating "V6X4258" to herself as she hurried into the house to write down the information.

"DMV Records. How can I help you?"

"Hello," Isabel said to the voice on the other end of the phone. "I'm trying to find the owner of a red Acura. I've got the license plate number."

"I'm sorry," the woman at the Motor Vehicles Bureau said. "We can't give out that information."

"But this is important. The car might belong to a missing person—someone who's been missing for a long time."

"Hold on, please," the woman said.

Isabel listened to soft music, interrupted occasionally by a message urging callers to access the Department of Motor Vehicles' website rather than wait on the telephone. Finally, she heard a click.

"Hello," a man's voice said. "You have a license plate number you think could belong to a missing person?"

"Yes."

"Please call your local police department and give them that information. They'll be able to track the license plate."

Before Isabel had a chance to respond, the man hung up.

The policeman Isabel spoke to didn't know anything about Nathan's disappearance. She wasn't surprised. The officer sounded very young and it had been twenty-five years. However, after checking the name "Nathan Goldsmith," he was eager to help.

"So your husband just vanished?" the policeman said.

"Yes."

"And you think you saw him today driving a red Acura?"

"Yes."

"Give me the license plate and I'll check it out."

Isabel read the number she had copied. She waited while he ran it through the computer.

After a couple of minutes, the officer returned to the phone.

"Nothing," he said.

"What do you mean?"

"The license plate you gave me doesn't exist. You must have copied it wrong."

"But I'm sure that was the correct number."

"I'm sorry, Mrs. Goldsmith," the policeman said. "There's nothing more I can do."

Isabel had trouble concentrating on her work the rest of the afternoon. Although she continued to sit in the backyard with her laptop, she spent the majority of the time wondering about Nathan. Finally she gave up and went inside.

For dinner she ate half a ham sandwich, not hungry enough to broil the flounder she had defrosted. *Nathan,* she kept thinking. *What's going on?*

It was nearly eight o'clock when the house phone rang. Isabel muted the TV, which she hadn't been watching anyway, and answered the call.

"Hi," her daughter Lainie said. "What's up?"

Isabel told her about the two Nathan sightings.

"Really?" Lainie asked. "You know that's impossible."

"Of course. But why am I seeing a man who looks like your father in a red car?"

"Like you said, because he disappeared twenty-five years ago today—and he always drove red cars."

Lainie had been away in college when it happened. Isabel had called her and explained that her father was missing. The girl had come home the next day and the two of them had worked together to try to find Nathan.

The police discovered his car in a small shopping center, twenty miles from home. But they found nothing else. A month later—after searches, posters, newspaper stories, and TV interviews—Isabel and Lainie had finally given up.

"I think about him every day," Lainie now whispered. "I still miss him."

"So do I," Isabel said, although she knew her comment wasn't true. She didn't miss Nathan at all, but Lainie, their only child, had been especially close to her father.

Isabel didn't mention the license plate number that didn't exist. Instead, she changed the subject. "How is everything with you?" she asked.

"Fine. Ed's going to get his raise and Mirella and Aiden are doing well in school."

Isabel's grandkids were eleven and nine and she did miss them. But, since Lainie's family lived in California, more than two thousand miles away, Isabel usually saw them just once or twice a year.

After several more minutes of small talk, Isabel ended the call. She watched some more TV, flipping channels, again without concentrating on what she was viewing. Then, at ten o'clock, feeling wiped out, she went to bed.

Isabel didn't sleep well. Her dreams were filled with images of Nathan—as a young man when she had first met him and then later, after they married and had Lainie. The dreams were mostly quick snapshots: Nathan would appear and quickly fade out before popping up again, like the opening montage in a wedding video.

She woke up at seven, exhausted and confused. After showering, Isabel poured herself a cup of coffee and stood at the kitchen counter, drinking, as she pondered her strange dreams.

Why won't he go away? Just leave me alone.

Isabel took another sip and glanced at the window over the sink. A red sports car was again parked across the street.

Isabel dashed out of the house, flinging open the front door as she ran, barefoot, towards the red car. Breathing heavily, she stood at the curb, staring at the car and the driver.

It was the same Nathan look-alike who now turned towards her. The man seemed to be talking, but she couldn't hear the words. However, she could make out his expression; he was frowning.

Cautiously, Isabel stepped into the street, frightened but curious about the mysterious man in the car. As she moved nearer, the man stopped talking, although he still scowled at her. Close-up, he looked exactly like Nathan! When she was just inches away, the man stepped on the gas and drove off.

Before the car faded into the distance, Isabel was able to read the license plate. It was V6X4258—the same number the policeman said didn't exist.

After her third sighting of Nathan in the red car, Isabel didn't even attempt to work. Instead, she tried to figure out what was happening. Was Nathan really back? But how could that be? He would be seventy-two years old, not this younger version. And why would he be driving that car?

When Nathan had vanished, he had also been driving a red Acura. He had told Isabel his clients loved riding in the sporty Acura to view houses. "It makes them feel special," he had explained. "Most agents have boring cars. This one adds excitement—and it increases sales."

Maybe he'd been right; Nathan had been a successful realtor and she and Lainie had lived a comfortable life. "Until that day in May," she whispered. That's when everything had changed.

◄◦►

Isabel didn't remember much after Maude had called about Nathan being missing. The rest of the day had been a blur of phone calls—to the police, to Lainie, to her parents, to Nathan's mother, to their friends—and then waiting for the call that Nathan had been found. But the call never came.

Then, after the search ended and everyone realized Nathan might never be found, she and Lainie had slowly settled into their new life. At first, it was quiet and sad, especially for Lainie, who spent the summer at home, moping aimlessly around the house and bursting into tears at odd times. The girl had tried working part-time in Sears, but quit after only two days on the job.

"I'm sorry, Mom," Lainie had said. "I keep thinking about Dad and forget what I'm supposed to be doing. I can't handle it."

Isabel had tried to be strong for her daughter, taking Lainie to dinner and the movies, and even for a short vacation at Lake Vinette. But that summer had been rough.

Things had improved after Lainie returned to Mount Holyoke for her sophomore year. Her friends and studies seemed to numb the loss of her father. At least, that's what Isabel hoped had happened.

For Isabel, it was as if a weight had been removed from her shoulders. Nathan had been bossy—telling Isabel what to cook and who to socialize with. If she had let him, he would have also told her what to wear and how to do her proofreading. She had chosen her battles, which is why they had compromised on the furniture.

It had taken lots of energy for Isabel to maintain any independence. She had fought hard for wardrobe control and professional freedom. However, she had allowed Nathan to dictate the dinner menu and arrange their social calendar.

When he disappeared, she had been free to plan her own meals and socialize with her own friends. Although she had never admitted it to Lainie or to anyone else, Isabel had felt greatly relieved.

Later that morning, Isabel decided to take a trip to the mall. *I can use another pair of jeans*, she told herself. But she knew the real reason: She needed to get away from her disturbing memories of Nathan.

Rose Cliff Plaza—an indoor grouping of stores on two levels, encircled by a large parking lot—was just a five-minute drive. Isabel reached the mall, parked, and walked inside.

As always, the bright fluorescent lights were disturbingly glaring. She blinked and headed for the escalator. When she stepped off the moving stairs, Isabel glanced below and there he was—the man who looked exactly like a younger version of Nathan.

He stood at the bottom of the escalator, scowling at her. Although the man seemed to be talking, again she was too far away to hear him. But this time she thought she could figure out what he was saying. It was just one word: "Why?"

Isabel raced to the down escalator and dashed to the bottom, taking two steps at a time. Despite her rush, when she reached the main level, the Nathan look-alike was nowhere to be seen. Once again, he had managed to vanish.

She stood in the center of the mall, arms on her hips, bewildered by the man. *How could he appear and disappear?* She needed to talk to him—to find out who he was and why he kept following her.

She sensed that the man wanted to talk to her too. But, if that were the case, why wouldn't he wait for her? Why did he keep driving away—or, like just now, running away?

She shook her head and walked slowly to the exit, in no mood to try on jeans.

At home, Isabel stood at her kitchen sink, clutching the countertop and trying to devise a plan. She couldn't work and she couldn't relax—all she could do was think about the Nathan look-alike who had invaded her life. Everything was on hold until she could speak to him.

She sat in the living room and gazed at the backyard. The man was there, leaning against the large maple tree and staring at her.

Isabel walked to the window and studied him. This time, he didn't look angry; he seemed perplexed. When he noticed her, he gave Isabel a small smile and signaled for her to join him.

Isabel didn't hesitate. She ran out the back door and headed toward the Nathan look-alike.

This time, the man didn't run away. "Who are you?" Isabel asked as soon as she reached him.

He ignored her question and continued to lean against the tree, appraising her. "You've gotten old," the man said. "Lots of wrinkles and age spots. You're shorter too—the incredibly shrinking woman."

He sounded just like Nathan, Isabel realized. *Even his sarcasm...*

"Who do you think I am?" the man asked.

"You look like my husband," Isabel said. "But he would be much older."

"Really?" The Nathan look-alike smiled at her.

"Yes. He was your age when he disappeared twenty-five years ago so he'd be in his early seventies today."

The man nodded, not smiling anymore. "That is correct." Then he scowled at Isabel. "If he was still alive."

Isabel took a step back. "You still haven't told me who you are."

"Do I have to?"

"What do you mean?"

"You know exactly who I am."

"No." Isabel shook her head. "I don't."

"All right then, I'll tell you." The man took a step towards Isabel. "I'm Nathan."

"You can't be."

"Why not?"

"I already told you. Nathan would be much older."

The Nathan look-alike laughed. But it wasn't a happy sound; it was a loud shrill roar. "You are amazing!" he shouted. "You really don't remember, do you?"

"Remember what?"

"What happened twenty-five years ago—when you murdered me."

Isabel dropped to her knees. "No," she said. "I didn't kill Nathan. He disappeared and I tried to find him."

The man shook his head. "You couldn't face what you did so you conveniently forgot. But I'm going to make you remember, whether or not you want to."

Isabel rose and walked backwards, but the man who claimed to be Nathan grabbed her wrists firmly and shoved her to the ground. "Sit!" he ordered. "Sit and listen."

Isabel felt the tears rolling down her cheeks as the man began talking.

"We had a fight that morning before I left for work. Do you at least remember that?"

"No," Isabel whispered.

"The fight was about Holly."

That name... Isabel had forgotten her. But now she was beginning to recall the woman.

"You found out that I was seeing her."

"'Seeing her?' You were sleeping with her—meeting in those empty houses."

Nathan stared at Isabel and nodded. "So you do remember. How about what happened after our fight?"

"You went to work..."

"You must have been watching me because, when I left for lunch, you followed me to the cabin where Holly was waiting. After she left, that's when you came in."

Isabel remembered. "And we had another fight and I picked up the onyx cat and..." She couldn't finish the sentence. She didn't want to remember the rest.

"Too messy for your sensitive mind?" Nathan asked. "You bashed my head with that stone—neatly, so there was no blood, but the force was strong enough to kill me."

The cabin, Isabel recalled, had been deep in the woods with no neighbors nearby so no one had seen or heard anything. It had also been on the market for such a long time, with no client interest, that the police never suspected Nathan had gone there.

Nathan had kept his affair secret so the police hadn't even questioned Holly and she hadn't volunteered she had been the last person to have seen Nathan alive. Maybe Holly had been afraid she would have been considered a suspect in his disappearance, or maybe she didn't want the negative publicity. She had been married with two young children.

After killing Nathan, Isabel had dragged the body into the woods. She had found a shovel in the shed and buried him, along with the onyx cat, covering the grave with leaves and sticks.

Then she had driven Nathan's car to a nearby strip mall and walked the mile or so back to the empty cabin in the woods to get her car. No one had noticed her—just a middle-aged woman taking a leisurely stroll on a beautiful spring day.

"Finally, you remember it all," Nathan said. "I can see it in your face."

"What are you going to do now?" Isabel asked, again backing away.

"It's not what I'm going to do. It's what you're going to do."

"And what is that?"

"You're going to confess to the police."

"No," Isabel said, shaking her head as the tears started flowing again. "I can't."

"You must."

"But what about Lainie?"

Nathan shrugged. "You should have thought about her feelings when you murdered me."

Isabel ran into the house and grabbed her keys. Then she raced to her car. She needed to drive somewhere—to a place far away from this Nathan-person.

She peeked into the rear-view mirror. Nathan wasn't following her. Isabel took a deep breath as she drove to the corner and continued until she reached the entrance to the highway.

Isabel didn't have a destination in mind. *Just clear my head until I figure out what to do.* He couldn't be real, this younger version of Nathan. *It's my brain,* she reasoned. All that stored guilt bubbling to the surface.

Isabel drove north, towards the country, and the traffic diminished until few cars were traveling in her direction. Someone behind her honked and when Isabel glanced in the rear-view mirror, she gasped. It was a red sports car and the driver, who smiled and waved, was the younger Nathan.

Isabel stepped on the gas pedal and drove faster, but the sporty red Acura zoomed past her, moving into her lane, in front of her car.

Isabel looked for an exit, but on this stretch of highway, there was nothing for miles. She slowed the car and Nathan did the same. She moved to another lane and Nathan, still ahead of her, drove into that lane too. Finally she gave up and continued driving at normal speed, determined to get off at the next exit.

The exit for Birchville was just two miles ahead when the red car in front of her came to a complete stop. Isabel, trying to swerve around the Acura, hit her brakes as hard as she could. But she was going too fast to avoid the inevitable crash. The last thing she saw was Nathan's face beaming at her.

"What the hell happened here?" the policeman said to his partner as they surveyed the crash site.

"It looks like the blue car smashed into the back of the red one," the woman said. "But why? This is an empty road."

The male officer reached inside what was left of the driver's side of the blue car and gently lifted Isabel's crushed head from the steering wheel. "She's dead," he said.

"Mac, take a look at this," his partner called from the red car.

"What?" Mac asked.

"There's nobody in here," the policewoman said. "How could that be?"

"Maybe the car stalled on the road and the driver left to get help," Mac suggested.

"I guess," his partner said. "But then she would have had plenty of time to see the car and avoid hitting it. It's bright red. How could she not have noticed it?"

"I don't know," Mac said. "Let's call in the license plate." He bent down and read the number. "Tell them to check out V6X4258."